L.A. STAFFORD

CHILD OF LIGHT

COMING SOON

BY L.A. STAFFORD

THE ANGELICS WIFE

From "Lay of the Minstrel"-
"Loves Nature"
"Love" (Canto III)
By Sir Walter Scott

In peace love proves the shepherd's reed,
In war, he mounts the warrior's steed;
In halls in gay attire is seen;
In hamlets, dances on the green.
Love rules the court, the camp, the grove,
And men below, and saints above;
For love is heaven, and heaven is love.

True loves the gift that God has given,
To man alone beneath the heavens;
It is not fantasy's hot fire,
Whose wishes, soon as granted fly;
That liveth not in fierce desire,
With dead desire, it doth not die;
It is the secret sympathy,
The silver link, the silken tie,
Which heart to heart and mind to mind,
In body and in soul can bind.

Michael erupted with rage, then drew his sword and attacked Jovan. He fought for his child, the woman he loved, for God and for his fellow Archangels. He fought for the Kingdom of Heaven and for humanity. The other Archangels appeared and stood side by side. His attack was ferocious, and Jovan began to weaken.

As Michael raised his sword to take Jovan's life, Metatron screamed, 'No Michael, God will be his judge!'

Michael grasped Jovan by the throat with one hand and placed his blade to Jovan's chest with the other. As they all appeared in front of God, Jovan glared at his maker.

'You dare to sit on that throne and command me?' he screamed at God.

'You think you have what it takes to command the Heavens, Jovan. I can see you have lost your way,' said God. 'I am your creator!' he screamed. Jovan's betrayal would now be his last.

Metatron moved closer to stand beside God. 'Jovan has killed a mortal and left this child without its mother.'

'I ask for justice, Father,' said Michael as he clenched his fist.

'Why don't you tell your maker who her father is, Michael?' Jovan yelled spitefully.

God waited for Michael's answer.

'She is my daughter,' said Michael.

'Yes, Michael, I know who she is. Bring her to me.'

Gabriel hesitated but did as God commanded. As God cradled her in his arms, He said, 'I will speak with Michael in a moment, however you, Jovan, my most beautiful of them all, how easily you fell. Your pride has shamed you. Your ego and jealousy have made you commit the greatest of all offences; to take a human life is the greatest of all sins. I hereby banish you from my Kingdom, never to return.'

As Jovan rose to his feet, he defied God's words and shouted, 'Oh, but I will. I will take your crown and sit on *my* throne. I will command the Heavens with Berenike by my side, and I will reign over the heavens and the dimensions within the universe.' He turned to Michael. 'I will rise again, and I will be watching her, Michael. I will always be watching. I promise you, I will come for her, and she will sit beside me, and I will rejoice in your pain as you watch me rule the heavens.'

The Archangels could see how angry Jovan was. He was no longer one of them. His hatred had transformed him from a being of light to a being of darkness. His lust for power had completely consumed him, and hate, arrogance, and deceit had become a part of him.

'Enough of this. Be gone from my Kingdom!' commanded God, raising his hand.

A crack of thunder echoed throughout the Heavens as Gabriel took Berenike back into his arms.

God observed the baby. 'This child is not to blame for the

actions of my wayward angels. I am, however, saddened by your loss, Michael. Sarra's death will be mourned by this Kingdom, and Jovan will not go unpunished.'

'Lord,' said Metatron, 'he will try again to take the Kingdom.'

'Yes, but not yet. We have some time,' He said. 'There is no doubt she is a child born of the light. What a unique situation this is. She is destined for many things. She will be the protector of my Kingdom. However, for the moment, Michael, your child will remain on Earth, where she will live and experience many lifetimes, protected. I grant her safe passage through the eons of time until Jovan comes for her. Then she will need to be ready.'

'Ready for what?' Michael asked.

'Jovan will try to take the Heavens from us again. He has worked out that she is a special child. She will have powers like we have never seen, and she will encompass both good and evil.'

'Evil … no!'

'Yes, with her mother being mortal, she will have the darkness of humanity within her. However, with the right guidance, we can ensure this does not come to pass.

'My Archangels, you will all watch over her and keep her from harm. I will surround her with Earth angels through each lifetime so she is protected.' He hesitated before he delivered the final blow. 'You must now say goodbye to her, Michael.'

'Please, no!' I

Michael took the baby into his arms. The thought of not being able to be near his child was unbearable. The Archangels were shocked at God's decision to send Berenike away. Michael would now lose the other love of his life, his daughter.

He pressed his cheek to hers and commanded Gaige, one of the warriors of his army, to be Berenike's protector through time, keeping her safe as they travelled together through many lifetimes.

Gaige was a strong, alert, and skilful warrior. He bowed his head to accept the command from Michael. Gaige was not an angel, but he was one of God's warriors, which would make his movement through the ages easier.

'You will stand by her side through each lifetime until the day we are reunited,' said Michael. Before he handed Berenike to Gaige, Michael whispered to his little girl, 'I will always be by your side. Whenever you're scared, I will be with you to give you strength.' He cried as he kissed his child goodbye.

'Safe passage, dear one. I will see you again, and I will watch over you as well,' said Gabriel. 'You will never be alone.'

'You will see her again, Michael.' Gabriel's reassurance was convincing.

The Archangels could feel Michael's sadness, and they would wait patiently through time until his daughter returned home.

CHAPTER ONE

THE WELL-MANICURED MAN

Berenike's day began like most. Her dreams had woken her like an alarm clock. The vision of a battle from a long time ago played over in her head like a broken record. She dressed for work, and as she left her house, she said goodbye to her beloved dog, Muffin. On the way to her shop, she picked up her usual coffee from the cafe next door.

Berenike owned a florist shop that also sold handmade chocolates and a large variety of sweets. Her clientele was anyone, from local children who would save their pocket money to buy her latest creations to business people who were trying to impress their partners. Her work gave her a chance to be creative while still making a living.

Berenike turned the open/close sign on the front door and returned to her work at the front counter. Soon, customer after customer flooded the store as her staff quickly tended to the needs of each one. It was going to be a busy day. As she stood at the counter, engulfed in paperwork, she had an uneasy feeling, and she looked up to see an attractive stranger staring back at her. His presence overwhelmed her, and his dark eyes held her stare. She felt a strange familiarity as she stepped back from the counter.

'I didn't mean to startle you. I was looking for someone.' His accent was different from anything she'd heard before.

'Oh, that's OK. I tend to get a little engrossed in what I'm doing at times and forget there's another world beyond the paperwork,' she said to the stranger.

He grinned. 'Indeed, there is. My name is Jovan. Is Berenike here?'

'I'm Berenike. I'm the owner,' she said proudly.

'Of course you are,' he said as he looked her over.

Berenike pushed the plate in front of him. 'Can I offer you a chocolate? I made them myself.'

Jovan had no choice but to be polite and accept the offer. He grinned. Her awkwardness showed as she leaned closer to him, trying hard to impress him.

Berenike noticed the man's striking looks and how his immaculate Armani suit encased his body. His hair was chocolate brown, his hands and fingernails were neat and tidy, and he smelt of Lagerfeld, her favourite men's aftershave. She smiled. He looked like he'd just stepped out of a glitzy fashion magazine. He was perfect.

'So, is there anything else I can help you with?' she said.

'No, I've found what I'm looking for.' Jovan's hypnotic stare made her feel dizzy, and he made her giggle with his charms. He stayed for several minutes, chatting.

'Angels and Sinners...what an interesting business name,' he said, grinning.

'Well, I've been told my chocolate is so good, it's sinful, and the floristry part comes from my love of flowers. Something that beautiful,' she said, 'would have to come from the Heavens above. A gift from God.'

'Yes, God indeed.' He laughed.

'You don't believe in G---'

Jovan cut her off mid-sentence. The last thing he wanted to do was listen to someone praise his creator. 'I've enjoyed our conversation Berenike. May I come back and see you?' he asked as he took another chocolate.

'Of course you can. I'd like that,' she replied blushing. His request to see her again was flattering.

'Well, until we meet again.'

He placed his hand on hers. At his touch, she received a flash of what seemed to be a memory of some sort – a memory from an ancient time, like in her recurring dream. There was ruin and destruction from a great battle.

Jovan's parting gift made her feel faint, and as she swayed, one of the staff ran to her aid. 'Are you OK? Here, sit down.' Linda dragged a chair towards Berenike, who was scared. The visions were becoming more frequent.

'I'm fine.' Berenike looked up to say goodbye to Jovan, but he'd disappeared amongst all the commotion.

Berenike welcomed closing time. She was exhausted.

'Can you both take some chocolate with you when you go? It's less on my hips,' she said to her staff. 'Thanks for working so hard. Sammy, here's a little something for your mother. Wish her Happy Birthday for me, won't you?' Sam came in after school for a few hours each day. He was the youngest member of her staff.

Berenike thought of him more as a younger brother than an employee.

'Thank you, Berenike, I will.' He hugged her and left.

Berenike noticed there was still a customer in the store. 'I'm sorry, but we're about to close for the day,' she said.

The customer said, 'Hi, I won't stay long. I saw what happened this morning, and I just wanted to make sure you were all right.'

'Thank you. Yes, I'm OK now. I just got a little lightheaded earlier. I'm more embarrassed that my staff had to see that,' she said. Berenike thought it odd this man had come back to the store specifically to see her. He didn't take his eyes off her, and an awkward silence passed between them.

'I've seen you in here before, haven't I?' Berenike said at last.

'I come here quite often. I like your little store,' the man said as he looked around the room. 'You've done well here.'

'Oh, thank you.' She wasn't sure where the conversation was going, but his concern for her seemed genuine. 'I didn't catch your name,' Berenike said.

The stranger smiled. 'Michael.'

'Well Michael, I'll look forward to seeing you next time.'

'Goodbye, Berenike,' he said as he left. She wondered how he knew her name.

Two in one day, girl. You're on a roll, she thought.

What a strange day. None of it made any sense, but she could not wait to get home. The events of the day had left her exhausted and uneasy. She could not shake the feeling something was not right. As she locked the shop door, she noticed a white feather on the floor. She ran the feather over her face before placing it on the counter.

'I hope I haven't got birds in the roof,' she said out loud, inspecting the ceiling.

CHAPTER TWO

DEATH

Berenike looked up into the night sky. As the stars shone bright, she made a wish on the brightest one she could see. She walked the length of the back yard. She could feel the grass stalks between her toes. The cold temperature and wet moisture on the grass soothed her feet, which were aching from standing up all day. Berenike wasn't afraid to put in the hard yards, but considering how exhausted she was from the constant reminder of days past, she knew she needed to rest.

As Muffin began to bark, Berenike made her way back into the house, stumbling and breathing heavily from the large amounts of alcohol she'd just consumed.

'Are you drunk, Muffin?' Muffin barked. 'Just as well.' She laughed. *I really should stop drinking,* she thought.

Muffin sat staring at what Berenike could see as nothing but thin air, her tail happily wagging back and forth. She didn't realise her fury companion could see the two Archangels standing before her.

'What are you looking at, Muffin? There's nothing there,' Berenike said as she kept staring into space.

'Don't you think it's time to tell her?' said Gabriel. He watched Berenike dance around the room until she was exhausted and fell onto the lounge.

'No, not yet. It's not time. She's not ready,' Michael said as he sat down beside his daughter.

'She'll never be ready if you don't tell her. He's already seen her today. He knows it's her, Michael.' Gabriel was concerned. The thought of her being defenceless had him very worried.

'Muffin, it's just us tonight,' Berenike said with a giggle.

She stood up from the lounge to change the music; she loved to unwind by dancing. As she stopped, her blue eyes widened as she caught a glimpse of another memory. The fear was overwhelming, and it made her freeze.

'She's having a vision, isn't she?' Gabriel said.

A loud knock at the front door startled Berenike back to reality.

'Who's come to visit?' she asked as Muffin territorially barked at the visitor behind the door. As her mystery guest knocked impatiently at the door, she heard a loud screech from the voice behind it.

'Will you open the door, woman?!' The voice from behind the door was familiar.

'No, you didn't do the thing.' With her hands on her hips, Berenike stood her ground.

'Oh, for goodness sake. You'd better have a drink waiting for me when I get in.' She knocked at the door again.

'Who's there?'

'Your worst nightmare if you don't let me in the damn door.' S

Berenike smiled as she opened the front door to find her best friend Amy standing there.

'Hello, gorgeous.' They both squealed, and Berenike hugged her friend. She was happy to see her. It had been a long week.

'Hell , Muffin dog, how are you?'

Muffin barked back. The response made them both laugh.

'I swear that dog is human,' Amy said as she scratched Muffin on the head.

'I like this human, Michael. She's very interesting,' said Gabriel. S

Michael's eyes widened as he looked Amy up and down.

'Look at the colour of her hair,' said Michael. is

Both Archangels sat there staring at Amy's vibrant red hair, which was the colour of a fire engine. Michael then decided it was time to go. His daughter was safe for the moment now that Amy had arrived.

'Come, Gabriel,' he said as he dragged his friend reluctantly away.

Amy was Berenike's best friend. Although Amy's red hair was a shock to many, Berenike loved how unique she was. She could have had purple hair, and it wouldn't have mattered. She loved her anyway. She was a strong woman and an even better friend. She was never cruel and loved Berenike like a sister.

Amy was very protective of her friend and had been observing over the last few weeks how withdrawn Berenike had become. Amy sat down on the kitchen bench and poured them both a drink. She decided now was a better time than any to approach her friend.

'So, is everything OK with you?' Amy asked.

'No, I'm drunk and dancing around the lounge room with my dog on a Saturday night. What do you think?' Berenike laughed. They both raised their hands to their foreheads to form the shape of an "L".

'That's not what I meant. Is anything bothering you? It's like you're all scattered.' Amy's hand gesture mimicked a swirl motion.

'I know. I just keep having this overwhelming feeling everything is speeding up around me. Like I'm racing to get somewhere. I've been having some strange dreams that are unnerving me, I guess. I fainted at work today too.'

The look on Amy's face matched the worry that had engulfed Berenike.

'Maybe you should see a shrink,' Amy said as she quickly drank the glass of wine. She was always blunt and straight to the point.

They both looked at each other and burst into laughter.

'OK, Dorothy, you don't need to see a shrink. You and your little dog will be just fine.'

Berenike laughed. 'Yes, we will. Anyway, are you heading in to town to meet EJ?'

'Yep, so do you want to put on something sexy and some dancing shoes?'

'Thanks, but I think I'll stay home tonight. I haven't had much sleep over the last few weeks.'

Amy could see she was exhausted. 'Good idea. Go to bed, and I'll call you in the morning.'

As Berenike walked Amy to the door, she hugged her friend.

'You know those dreams? They'll pass. You need to get more sleep and stop working so hard. You have staff to do that, remember? Take a day off,' Amy suggested.

Berenike nodded in agreement. Amy was right, she needed to rest.

'Get some Zs my friend. I love you.'

'I love you too,' Berenike said as she hugged her friend goodbye.

The thoughts of the day were starting to flash repeatedly in her mind. It was bothering her that so many unanswered questions had come out of the day's events.

'Well, my little one, I think it's time to rev this party up a little.' Berenike turned up the volume on her stereo. 'Let's have one last dance before bed.'

Berenike noticed another feather on the floor. 'That's strange; at home as well.' She stumbled around the lounge room and knocked into the side arm of the chair. 'Ouch!'

As she poured another glass to finish the bottle, her intoxication began to dull the pain of the visions she was experiencing. Jovan appeared from behind the veil and sat on the arm of the chair, watching her.

'Bottoms up,' he said, laughing as Berenike drank to the bottom of the glass.

As Berenike walked back into the lounge room, she slipped on the floor rug that lay across the polished timber floor. Her wine glass flew into the air and smashed as it reached the floorboards. As she fell, her head hit the timber floor and she closed her eyes for the last time as a human being.

A crack of thunder alerted the Heavens that Berenike was on her way home. s

Michael smiled as his fellow Archangels surrounded him. 'It's time.'

Muffin jumped on Berenike's slumped body. The small dog began to whimper as a pool of blood started to grow on the floor.

'I'll see you soon, Berenike,' said Jovan.

Muffin growled at Jovan. She may have only been a small dog, but she would protect Berenike every way she knew.

Jovan backed away from her loyal companion and disappeared into the darkness.

CHAPTER THREE

HEAVEN

Berenike's vision slowly darkened until there was nothing but black. As she floated through the darkness of the void, her vision was filled with light. Berenike felt the touch of a hand as it grasped hers. She could feel her hand being pulled as it guided and lifted her body into the light. As she entered the Kingdom of Heaven, she saw the most beautiful beams of crystal white light within her vision. The warmth of the rays rested on her face as the most overwhelming feeling of peace swept over her. She passed through several rooms of white. Empty rooms with no doors. White on the inside and the outside. As her eyes explored her surroundings, she was standing in a white abyss.

An overwhelming feeling of love embraced her as she drew breath into her lungs. The being that had been guiding her led her past many doorways and through room after room. The entire surroundings were white, with a neon glow and a tinge of blue. The walls were as tall as the sky and went on as far as the eye could see.

The spirit turned to her, and as she heard a voice in her head, she listened.

'This is where I have to leave you. Be strong. I am always with you.'

'Who are you? Don't go! Come back!'

Berenike stood alone in silence. Her skin began to tingle as she felt a presence standing beside her. Her fear began to hasten her breathing.

'Who's there?' She swung around to see what was behind her. She felt many eyes watching her.

As the room slowly filled, Berenike was confused by what she was seeing. Her eyes squinted together as her white surroundings slowly disappeared and her sight found its clarity. In front of her was a constant traffic flow of angelic beings. Not all looked like angels. There were animals, children and adults of all ages before her. Some had wings, and some were floating in the air.

As she glanced around before her, she saw the familiar face of a man she had encountered earlier in the day. He walked towards her, smiling. His pale blue suit jogged her memory; it was the same suit he'd appeared in earlier.

'Oh, you have got to be kidding.'

As he moved closer towards her, she felt a sense of warmth in her heart.

'Welcome home, Berenike. I'm Michael. Do you remember?' he said as he formally introduced himself. She nodded yes.

'You were in my store today.' She laughed out loud. 'I really need to give up drinking. This is going to be one hell of a hangover when I wake up.'

'Yes, well, we can talk about that later.' Berenike raised her eyebrow at his remark. 'We didn't expect you here this soon.'

'Here? We? What do you mean?' Berenike was confused

enough with what she had just experienced. She had no idea where she was.

'Child, you're in Heaven.'

She placed her hand to the side of her head and began to rub at the pain that was increasing. 'I have a headache.'

Michael raised his hand to touch her forehead. As he gently touched her, her headache disappeared.

No sooner had he spoke, the Archangels appeared before them. Michael smiled at his friends. They were eager to welcome the lost child of Heaven back into the fold.

As they all appeared to her, they made quite the sight. Metatron was a tall figure whose mere presence was commanding. He had been the hardest of them all to convince it was safe to accept Berenike as a part of their family years ago. The years had softened his heart toward her, and he eagerly awaited her arrival back in Heaven, just as the others had. The time that had separated them all from her had healed their fear at the mere thought of a being like Berenike.

Metatron had dark skin and was of solid build. He was different from the other Archangels. Physically, he looked older than they did, and his face was fatherly, which immediately put her at ease.

Gabriel appeared before them and stood back from the others and observed while trying to contain his excitement. Gabriel had watched her through many of her lives and cradled her in his arms when she was a baby. He moved slowly behind the group. Berenike felt a nervous pull in the centre of her heart. Gabriel was happy she was finally here and found it quite difficult to contain his emotions as his feet shuffled in the background.

Gabriel was also quite tall, with mousy blonde hair like her own colour. He had strikingly beautiful blue eyes and thin lips. His chiselled good looks made her blush, and as he caught her eye, he smiled.

She fascinated Raphael. He had never been this close to her before, as the veil between Heaven and Earth had always separated them. He carried a little more weight than the others. He had red hair, which made her smile, and was a jolly fellow with a sense of humour to match, as Berenike would soon discover. His armour plating sat proudly over his chest as he stood tall with the others. She noticed they all seemed to be over 6ft tall, were statuesque and extremely striking, radiating an unintentional beauty.

As Raphael moved closer towards her to offer an embrace, she took a step back and hid behind Michael. His sudden movement towards her left her startled.

'Back off, bird.'

Her fierce statement had Raphael proceeding with caution, and he did as she asked. He could see he'd frightened her. He gracefully bowed his head to her, and she observed his Archangel wings as they were folded into the centre of his back.

'I did not mean to frighten you, child,' Raphael's voice softened as he explained. 'It's just that we've been waiting for you to join us for such a long time. This is quite exciting for us to have you here. I am Raphael.'

'I'm sorry, I didn't mean to call you bird.'

Metatron laughed at her comment. 'My name is Metatron. Welcome home, Berenike.' He bowed to her.

Uriel had been standing back observing as well, his arms aggressively folded. 'Do you think she has what it takes? Michael, you haven't told her, have you?'

Uriel's voice boomed. Berenike found it quite irritating as her face screwed up in irritation. The Archangels spoke in a higher frequency than most humans were used to. It was loud and painful.

Uriel was skeptical, and it was obvious Berenike would have to prove herself to him. She was no longer the baby he'd observed many years ago. She was a grown woman now.

'Told me what? And who are you?' Berenike's facial expression soured as she stood strong and directed the comment to him. Uriel could see he'd made her feel terribly uncomfortable. Her face was angry.

'My name is Uriel.' Uriel smiled at her as a form of peace offering. Uriel's presence was quite overpowering. He had dark brown hair, was tall like the others and was very attractive, which made him extremely intimidating to her. Uriel had just made a very poor first impression on her.

'Hello.'

'Uriel, she just arrived,' Michael explained. 'Jovan came to see her this morning. She's been having flashes from the past, and they've almost crippled her.'

Michael could feel how nervous she was. As Berenike observed the beings standing before her, she recognised all their names. They were all dressed in ancient suits of armour, except Michael, who had remained clothed in his suit, more so for Berenike to feel at ease with him. She could see their armour was regal. There were crystals planted into the armour, and the plating was white, which glistened like a new star. The armour appeared to be slightly different with each Archangel. They were all individual and unique. A mix of crystal and metal reflected on the ancient words etched into the chest plating, and Berenike would later learn the words were Aramaic, although she already assumed they were the words of God. She could also see they all had large wings like birds. They appeared to her in their angelic form. She was standing in the presence of God's Archangels.

Metatron's wings were beautiful, as were the others. Shades of grey and white, with his body glowing gold. They were all tall of stature, solid and masculine and incredibly beautiful.

Gabriel had been watching everything unfold. Berenike blushed as he smiled at her again. She could not take her eyes off him. Gabriel was beautiful, and just the mere sight of him softened her eyes. He stood aside from the others as he watched her. The more she looked him over, the more nervous she felt. Berenike wasn't the type of girl who'd ever stood out with any man, but she was now centre stage.

Berenike listened as they argued over her and debated the course she should take next. She tried to listen to what was going on but found their words very confusing as the conversation became heated. Each Archangel provided an opinion on what guidance would be best. The muffling sound of their voices all at once was irritating. She placed her hands to her ears to block out the noise of their arguing and began to run.

'Whoa, where are you going?' She ran straight into Gabriel. He could sense the anxiety growing within her.

'This must be a lot for you to take in right now.'

She wasn't sure what to say, so she nodded yes. Gabriel led her to a quiet area close by, still within Michael's sight, so he could speak with her.

'Your senses will adjust to your surroundings. Be patient.'

'You're an angel, aren't you?' she said.

'I'm an Archangel, just like the others. My name is Gabriel.'

Berenike looked into Gabriel's eyes and investigated every section of his face. It was her turn to make him nervous. He swallowed hard as she made direct eye contact with him.

'I've known you for a very long time.'

'Really, how?' She was curious.

'I know your father; he is a dear friend.'

'And my mother?'

'She was the one who took your hand and led you here. She is always with you, as are we. Your mother's name is Sarra.'

'And what about my father?'

Gabriel smiled at her question but left it unanswered. Gabriel had no sooner finished speaking when the Archangels, including Michael, were all anxious to hear the conversation.

'The man who came into my store today was looking for me. His name was Jovan.'

'He was once one of us but is now one of the fallen. We do not speak of him.'

'Fallen? You mean one of the Angels that rebelled?' Gabriel was surprised she even remotely knew anything about Heaven and the Archangels. 'You mean that actually happened?'

He smiled. 'Yes, Berenike, it did, but how do you know about us?' asked Michael.

'Oh, you guys are very popular,' she said sarcastically. Berenike found the entire conversation amusing.

Metatron was becoming impatient. 'Tell her, Michael.' We are running out of time. You know he's built an army. He will come for her.' Michael was hesitant but decided it was indeed time to tell his daughter the truth.

'So, what does he want with me? I own a chocolate shop and a florist. What's he got, an excessive sweet tooth or something?' She couldn't help laughing and folded her arms.

Michael hesitated before he spoke. 'He can use you as a vessel of pure light and destroy God with the intent of taking over his Kingdom,' said Michael. 'You possess the light of God within you. It is the most powerful force in the universe besides the love of God. You are the light, child.'

'OK.' Everyone was silent as she looked at one Archangel after another. 'You're serious, aren't you?'

'Berenike you must understand, your time on Earth in your Earthly body has now passed. There is no going back.' Her eyes widened as she began to panic. The expression on Michael's face scared her.

'I can't go back. What are you talking about?'

She looked to Gabriel for answers. His lips were pursed together, and she could see the concern on his face. To some extent, they had forgotten how hard it could be for some human beings to accept an afterlife, let alone the concept of Heaven.

'I'm dead?'

'Not exactly. As I said, you have ceased to exist in that form,' explained Michael. 'Your spirit is still alive, of course. You have now reached a higher level of consciousness. Berenike, I think you need to come with me.'

As she turned her back on him and walked away, Michael appeared in front of her again.

'I am not going anywhere with you. I want to go home!'

Before Berenike realised it, Michael had reached for her arm. In the blink of an eye, she appeared to be back in her home. She stared down at herself as her body lay slumped on the floor in a pool of blood. As her former self lay motionless, she bent down to get a closer look. She examined every section of her face and was distressed at the bruising she could see on the side of her head from where her head had hit the floorboards.

'I'm so still.'

As Berenike looked down at her hands, she noticed a brilliant white glow surrounding her body. She was dressed in a long, flowing, soft white gown. Her sandy blonde hair flowed softly down over her shoulders. Berenike slowly looked over her clothing as she realised her garments were those from Heaven.

'She looks like her mother, Michael.' Jovan appeared and circled Berenike.

'So, where's your wings?' she said.

'Higher beings like myself don't need wings.'

'You're not a higher being! You live in the sewers of Hell!' Michael shouted.

'Michael, we both know that's only temporary. Come, old friend, join me, and we can rule together.'

Jovan glanced back at Berenike.

'I didn't expect her to be so beautiful. She is of the light.'

Jovan could sense the light from within her, a light he had not felt in over a thousand years. He closed his eyes and raised his hand before him, as if to drain all the energy from within her. Michael knew she would be in danger around him. As Jovan reached out to touch her hair, Michael drew his sword and pulled Berenike toward him. Jovan was hypnotised by the energy she was radiating. It was as if he was looking at the light for the very first time.

'I'll die before I let her stand by your side,' said Michael.

Michael was worried. Jovan had appeared to Berenike several times now. He knew he would be preparing for the battle to take control of the Heavens and destroy his maker.

'It's time to go, Berenike,' Michael said, then disappeared with his daughter.

CHAPTER FOUR

KINGDOM

Darkness echoed from one end of Hell to the other. Fire and darkness were as normal in Hell as the light was to Heaven. The city was trapped in a perpetual shade of darkness. From one side to the other, the sky was shades of burnt orange and red. Jovan's throne room resembled a dungeon with a single chair situated in the centre of the room. It was quite elaborate looking in shades of brown and rust. He had lived in Hell since the day God banished him from Heaven.

Jovan had established his own Kingdom, where he commanded all things dark. He would control the many souls throughout the chambers of Hell, with the torment and pain they had inflicted in their human lives. As he sat on his throne, his presence was commanding, yet many of his followers, in fear of him, all wanted to please their King. His tall stature and overbearing presence made him appear quite the enemy.

After visiting Berenike, and his run-in with Michael, Jovan was troubled more than usual. Berenike was weighing heavily on his mind.

'Sire, did you see her? What was she like?' Minion asked. 'Will she be our Queen?'

Jovan remained in a dream state as he spoke. 'She was beautiful; she is of God,' he said quietly to himself. 'She was shining with a glow I have not seen in a very long time. I could almost feed off her light. She was everything I expected her to be, being the daughter of Michael. It will not be easy to separate her from him. The bond has already formed.'

Jovan left from his throne and walked across to the window. He stared out into the surroundings of Hell. As he looked out and into the horizon of fire, he began to contemplate how he was going to defeat Michael and capture Heaven.

'Michael is the key. I need to defeat him and his army. Then it will be easy to take her and bring her here.'

'I would think you would be better off just to set your sights on winning her over, Sire.'

'Either way, my friend, we take Heaven and all its occupants, and we will create my world, the world of Jovan. The world that should have existed centuries ago.'

'You will need to seduce her, Sire, make her feel wanted and important to get her on your side. Play on her ego. Make her feel you are the only man for her and you can give her anything she has ever wanted. Seduce her, and you will be irresistible to her.'

'Of course I will. I won't need to seduce her; I am irresistible,' said Jovan.

Minion smirked. He was extremely patient. Over the centuries, he had dealt with Jovan in a father and son like manner, giving him counsel and direction whilst manipulating Jovan in a way that allowed Minion still to keep secret control of him. Minion knew from the moment he met Jovan, he would be easy to manipulate. Jovan was extremely immature, childlike at times, and Minion found it easy to persuade him.

'Once you have her under your control, then you will have the weapon you need. Defeat him, and you control the Kingdom, for only Berenike and the light within her can destroy the Kingdom of God. Then we will have the Kingdom of Jovan.'

Minion was corrupt. He was the perfect mentor for Jovan. His constant voice of evil and power that oozed from him was pleasing to Jovan's ears.

'She will need to come here voluntarily, Sire; you must not bring her here by force, or it will all fail.'

'She will come.'

Minion was curious. 'Sire, why have you not taken a Queen before?'

'There has never been anyone worthy until now, Minion.' Jovan almost looked at Berenike like a challenge. 'She's a woman;_it won't take long to convince her she belongs with me, where she can use her powers and not have to hide her unique abilities from the world. She can use her powers to control humanity. I'll see to that.'

'Is she smart, Sire? Because if she is, she won't be that easily influenced. You need to get to the heart of what she loves the most, find out what that is and then seduce her with it.' Minion was intelligent enough to know just because she was a woman, it would not deem her as stupid.

'Don't underestimate her, Sire.' He frowned. Minion was concerned with his attitude.

'What she loves the most is her family and friends, especially those on Earth.'

Minion could see him plotting and scheming, and he loved it. He loved that side of Jovan when he exuded evil.

'What do you propose, Sire?'

'I need to talk to her alone, away from Michael.'

'How do you intend on finding her?' Minion's curiosity was overflowing.

'I'll find her.'

CHAPTER FIVE

GOODBYE

Within seconds, Archangel Michael had transported himself and Berenike away from Jovan, to the location of Berenike's casket.

'It's white!' Berenike was surprised. 'At least someone has a little bit of taste. Am I really in there?' As she took a closer look at her coffin, she felt a chill over her skin.

'Why is it human beings are so shocked when they die? We tell you you're dead, and you still don't believe us,' said Michael.

'Oh, I don't know, maybe it's because you take our lives from us, our loves, and the people we care about.'

Michael's demeanour changed toward her. Seeing he was hurt by the comment, Berenike slowly walked around the casket, challenging Michael like a child.

'Look in there if you don't believe me,' he suggested.

Berenike jumped on top of her casket and swung her legs back and forth, glaring at Michael. He knew she was testing him.

Berenike was upset she was dead, and Michael was her closest target. The parent and child dynamic had just begun.

'Well, this should be interesting.' Berenike's glare softened as she saw her friends.

Guests arrived and began to take their seats. As most of the guests knew each other, everyone did the customary meet and greet. Amy wanted things to run smoothly, but her anger began to erupt at the sight of Gaige. Berenike had loved Gaige, but the relationship between them had left her heart broken. He hadn't treated her with the respect she deserved. His cheating and infidelities when they were together were a harsh betrayal for her to accept, as she thought she was the only woman in his life, his one and only love. Gaige had been living a human life, but he was neither human nor angel; he just was. As the many years passed, Gaige himself learned to adjust to life on Earth with Berenike at his side. Without the guidance of the Archangels, Gaige was left to his own devices, and that included Berenike.

As heads turned towards Gaige, Amy proceeded down the aisle of the church and straight toward him. With one swing, Amy slapped Gaige across the face with the intensity of a missile. Her grief had gotten the better of her. Without a word, she turned on her heels and stormed away from him.

EJ looked on and did nothing. Michael knew Gaige and Berenike had been together, and this made him extremely unhappy. Amy's reaction had certainly gained Michael's attention. Gaige would have to suffer her anger if he wanted to pay his respects to Berenike.

Berenike saw Amy in the distance and jumped off her casket. She walked towards her friend and sat with her as she cried. Berenike watched Amy deal with the proceedings.

'Amy, you don't have to do this.'

Amy's face was the saddest she'd ever seen. As the proceedings took place, Berenike moved from one side of the room to the other, watching her friends during the service. As she stood there observing, she could see the sadness within each heart. Being dead gave her a whole new perspective on life itself. She felt grateful so many people had come to acknowledge her and say goodbye.

'Berenike, it's time to go.'

She was finally in agreement with Michael. She knew it was time. 'Just, let me say goodbye.'

Michael nodded yes.

Berenike noticed that while EJ was thanking everyone for their attendance, Amy had slipped away from the crowd, stealing a few quiet moments for herself and her friend as she sat by Berenike's casket. Berenike knelt in front of Amy. She remained silent and watched her friend, who was completely engulfed in her own grief. Michael listened as she finally spoke.

'I wish I could take the sadness from your heart, my friend. Thank you for loving me,' she said.

'You can,' he said. 'You can give her peace. She will not forget you are gone, but the sadness will not be so crippling for her. Amy is grieving painfully. Here, let me show you.' Michael bent down in front of Amy. 'Place your hand near her heart and just think about what you want to give her.'

'I want her to be at peace when she thinks of me,' Berenike said.

Michael nodded his head to grant the command, then Berenike's hand glowed a bright and intense light towards her friend. Amy stood up and walked to Berenike's casket. They both stood side by side, as they always had.

'If you can hear me, I just want you to know, I love you and I will see you again my friend,' Amy said, then kissed her fingers and touched the top of the casket.

'I love you too,' Berenike whispered as Amy left.

As Berenike watched Amy and EJ leave the church, her eyes filled with tears. She felt alone for the first time in a very long time. As the doors to the church closed behind Amy and EJ, so did the life Berenike once knew. She stood in front of Michael and looked to him for comfort, and he reached out to embrace his daughter as her sadness softened his heart. She rested her head against his chest. He could hear Berenike sniffing as she hid her face to drown out the sound of her tears.

'I'll take you home.' Michael cradled his daughter in his arms.

As Michael closed his eyes, they appeared back in the surroundings of Heaven.

'Why don't you look around and get familiar with everything?'

She nodded, then walked the grounds of what she viewed as a city. The Kingdom of God was a spectacular sight. The one thing that stood out to her was the smiles and happiness of those who had passed.

'The community of Heaven,' she said, shaking her head. 'Those still on Earth have no idea it all exists.'

As Michael stood back watching her, Gabriel approached him and observed.

'It's wonderful having her here among us. I must admit, Michael, I thought it would never happen. How is she?'

'She's had a rough day. I thought she should get to know her surroundings a little better, so she's taking a walk. Gabriel, he's come to her twice now. He won't stop until he has her.'

'He tried to touch her, didn't he?' Michael could hear the protectiveness in Gabriel's tone of voice.

'Yes.' Michael frowned. 'It's interesting how after all this time, he's still attracted to the light.'

'What do you mean?' Gabriel was curious.

'It was odd watching him with her. She was not scared of him. He is evil. His mere presence was seductive to her. I could barely stand to be near him, yet she was comfortable in his presence. It may have been the light or just the fact that she is half-human. God did say she would have the perfect balance of good and evil, meaning she has a dark side as well. Every human has that darkness within them. I'm just glad she is far more angelic than the other.'

'Then we need to protect her. Don't worry, Michael, she takes after her father.'

Michael smiled. 'Thank you, my friend,' he said.

Michael decided to join his daughter. As he walked throughout the Heavenly palace, his blue suit slowly disappeared as it morphed into a white angelic suit of armour, like the other Archangels, complete with crystal and the words of God etched into the chest plating. His wings remained tucked behind his back. His hair was short and showed many strands of grey, which made his appearance quite mature. Michael was an attractive being with a heart that was even more beautiful than his looks. The blue aura surrounding him made his stature visibly regal. Michael stood out as the leader of God's army. He not only looked the part of a leader, with his sword attached to his waist belt, he oozed authority and cut quite the handsome figure.

Although still unaware he was her father, Berenike felt an unspoken closeness to him. She felt safe when he was near.

Berenike watched the children play, laughing and smiling as they ran and played with their pets that had joined them. It truly was a place of happiness. She observed lost friends and family members seeing each other for the first time in years. In the distance, she could see the most beautiful field of flowers. All the different colours of the rainbow. They were vibrant, and the intensity of the flowers lit up the sky with their magnificent glow.

As she walked barefoot through the corridors of the palace, Berenike stepped through the doorway into an old library of books and ancient writings. The books went from the floor all the way up into an endless sky. There were too many to see where they finished. There were bays and bays of books as far as the eyes could see and beyond.

As she explored the Holy Palace, she ventured out further. She walked out onto what was a huge marble floor with an open balcony leading out to the most spectacular mix of colour she'd ever seen in the skies. Pink, purple, and blue, and in the centre of the colour was pure gold radiance. Heaven had unveiled itself to her, and it was magnificent.

'Oh my.' Her heart skipped a beat. As Berenike looked out into the sky, she closed her eyes to feel the light of Heaven on her face. 'So this is what it's like...so this is Heaven.'

She could feel the grace of God amongst the rays of the horizon as the energy from the rays cupped her face within its hands, and for that one moment its beauty paralysed her. The love she felt from it was like nothing she'd ever felt before.

As Berenike closed her eyes, she could hear Michael's footsteps. When he stopped and stood beside her, she could sense his presence.

She opened her eyes. 'Why are you looking at me like that?'

'I've never seen anyone feel his light like you do.'

'It feels warm.'

Michael smiled. She reminded him of her mother. She had the same gentle smile as Sarra. He knew it would be hard not to love her.

'You know, I think this will be my favourite place.'

As they both looked out across the horizon, she could see a sky full of Angels, basking in the rays of the light.

'Then it will be mine too.'

She smiled to herself at his comment, then looked deeper into the light. 'What are they doing?'

'Exactly what you're doing.'

'I can hear them singing. I've never heard anything like that before. It's beautiful.'

The melody from the beings in front of her touched her soul as she smiled. She reached over to hold Michael's hand, and her affectionate gesture surprised him. He took a deep breath as he squeezed her hand.

In the distance, Gabriel and Uriel were watching. With Uriel being the stern but sensible Angel he was, he could see the bond forming between the two of them. He couldn't help grinning as he addressed Gabriel.

'Let them talk for a while. She's obviously warming to him. Whether we like it or not, she is his daughter,' said Uriel.

'I can't imagine what it must be like for him never to have been able to hold his child in his arms. All those years just watching her.' Thinking about the sacrifice Michael had made to keep Berenike safe all those years made Gabriel sad.

'You talk like he's human. Gabriel, she's not supposed to exist.'

'But she does. She's home now, so get used to it!' Gabriel snapped.

Uriel was quite shocked at the outburst from him. Gabriel was not an aggressive being, but when it came to Berenike, Uriel knew Gabriel would die for her. He was extremely protective of her. After having to hide behind the veil for many centuries and then finally being close enough to touch her, he knew it would be an adjustment.

'I've always understood Jovan's envy where Berenike is concerned, but more so now.'

Uriel understood Gabriel's comment and just nodded. He observed Michael and Berenike to see them deep in conversation whilst basking in the Heavens. Michael's love for his daughter had touched them all.

'Gabriel, how long do you think you can fool everyone?'

'What are you talking about?' Gabriel snapped at him.

'I've seen how you look at her. We have all seen how you watch her. You're in love with her.'

Gabriel was alarmed; his secret was now exposed.

Uriel continued. 'I guess you have spent the most time with her out of all of us, including Michael. Of all the people to fall in love with, Gabriel.' Uriel shook his head. 'Go carefully, there, won't you?' Uriel smiled as he patted Gabriel on the back. 'Don't forget, Michael is her father, and you are also his friend.'

'It's so beautiful here. I don't think I've ever felt peace like this before,' said Berenike.

'No, you wouldn't have. This peace, you only feel here in God's Kingdom; that's why it's so special. This is your home now.' He could sense the sudden sadness within her. She nodded accepting her new surroundings. Michael gently took her hand. 'Berenike, I have something important to tell you.'

No sooner had he spoke, Metatron appeared. 'It's time for training,' he said, excited.

'What, Angel training?' Berenike said.

'Come with me, dear one.' Gabriel took Berenike to change into her uniform. 'You're going to love this.'

'Really?'

'Oh, yes.'

Gabriel and Berenike both giggled at each other. She enjoyed being near him now that her nerves had settled down.

'Did we interrupt something, Michael?' said Metatron.

'Actually, I was about to tell her.' Metatron could see how nervous Michael was.

'You haven't told her yet you're her father?' asked Uriel. They were all losing patience with him.

'We just had a run in with Jovan. She saw her body today at her funeral, and she said goodbye to her friends. It's a lot for her to deal with. The time just wasn't right. Not yet anyway.'

CHAPTER SIX

COMBAT

Gabriel and Berenike chatted while she put on her uniform. As Berenike changed, Gabriel strutted around nervously. Berenike's uniform was white like Gabriel's and had its own special kind of armour. It was unique but very feminine.

She appeared from behind the screen in her room. 'Have I got this on right, Gabe?' she asked as she struggled with one of the straps that draped over her shoulder.

Her uniform fit her beautifully as it hugged her figure. He couldn't take his eyes off her. Gabriel was extremely attracted to her. 'Yes, you have it on right. Perfect.' He struggled to get the words out as he cleared his throat.

'So, this is like boot camp for Angels, right?'

As Gabriel fussed over her in preparation, he grinned at her sarcastic comment. 'Here is where we see how much of what you possess is instinct or if we need to completely train you. You need to be ready for Jovan. You're already aware he will come after you?'

'Yeah, I've worked that one out. I'm the child of the light!' she gushed. Her comment made him laugh, and she smiled at him as she felt the warmth of his smile.

'You have a beautiful smile.' Her words made him stand a little taller. He continued to straighten the straps that had fallen from her shoulders.

'I'm surprised you didn't take self-defence classes or train in martial arts while you were on Earth.'

'Maybe I did in a past life or something?'

'No, you didn't. I would have seen it if you had.'

Berenike thought about his comment. 'What do you mean I would have seen it? Have you been watching me?' Gabriel face remained expressionless. Berenike's eyes widened. 'Well, just what did you see?'

'Oh,' he paused, 'everything,' he said with a giggle. He grinned as he teased her.

'You are completely icky, mister. One word, boundaries!' she yelled as loud as she could at him.

'I was looking out for you, trying to protect you!' Gabriel yelled back at her.

Michael entered the room to see an extremely heated argument between the two of them. 'What's going on here?' He was distressed at the sound of his daughter and best friend fighting.

'Nothing,' they both yelled as they walked away from each other.

'What did you just say to her? Why is she so angry, Gabriel?' Michael demanded to know what he'd said to his daughter.

'I may have just accidently told her I've been keeping an eye on her all these years.'

'OK, and the rest?'

'I may have said I've been watching her instead of keeping an eye on her.' Gabriel bowed his head.

'What?!'

'It just came out all wrong. I'm sorry, Michael.'

As Gabriel explained, Michael could sense his upset from Berenike's harsh words. 'There were times I was so worried, I just couldn't leave her side. Times when I wasn't supposed to be watching, I had to.' Michael's anger subsided as he realised how much Gabriel really did care for his daughter. 'Michael, she called me icky.' Gabriel was terribly upset at Berenike's comment. She'd wounded his pride. He bowed his head.

'You my friend are far from icky.' Michael laughed. 'OK, enough. I'll go and get her.'

As Gabriel prepared the equipment for training, Michael decided to smooth things over between his friend and daughter. As he approached Berenike, he could see the argument had bothered her as well. She was hurt they'd argued. She really liked Gabriel, and the bond between the two of them was growing at a rapid rate.

'Don't be angry at him for too long. Gabriel loves you very much. He is probably the most emotional of us all when it comes to you. He has been with you for a long time. Many centuries, in fact. You know, sometimes as an Archangel, we see things we do not want to, but he is right, it is our job, and it was his to watch you. Will you go and talk to him, please?'

'All right.'

She took a deep breath as she approached the Archangel and stood before him.

'Gabe, can we talk?' Gabriel sat in silence.

'I didn't mean to react like that. I was just shocked. I'm sorry I said that to you.' Gabriel kept sharpening his sword, listening as she spoke. 'You're not icky at all. I think you're beautiful.' She had his attention. 'Don't tell anyone, but you're my favourite Angel,' she said, smiling. 'Will you forgive me?'

Gabriel put his sword down, reached over to her, and slipped his hand around her waist. Her heart began to race as he moved her body in closer to his chest. He could not remove the grin on his face as he kissed her on her forehead.

'Already forgiven.'

She threw her arms around his neck and hugged him as tightly as she could. Michael smiled, watching in the distance as he shook his head at the two of them and laughed to himself.

Metatron, Raphael and Uriel entered the combat room. As they all gathered around Berenike, Michael explained what was about to happen. Gabriel decided he would be the first.

'Berenike, remember what I just told you. We want to see how much is instinct, so just go with it.'

Berenike nodded in agreement of the instruction, then began to swing her sword in defence as the Archangels all proceeded to attack her with full force. By the end of the session, she was exhausted.

'Michael, I need to stop,' she pleaded. They'd knocked her over several times.

'Berenike, get up. Do you think Jovan will let you take a break?' said Metatron, who glanced over at Michael. He knew of Metatron's goal to push her and bring forth the light residing dormant within her. 'Get up!' Metatron yelled, then swung his sword, narrowly missing her.

Berenike jumped to her feet, swung her sword, and knocked Metatron off balance. As he fell straight to the floor, Michael beamed with pride. The fighting instinct they were hoping for was starting to emerge. They could all see there was strength there, and with guidance she could possibly outskill them all.

'Well done, child. Now I want you to stand back and just watch.'

Michael nodded to both Gabriel and Metatron. Their plan was about to be unleashed, and if all went as expected, it would unleash Berenike as well.

Gabriel and Metatron skilfully demonstrated the art of combat. The clanging of swords became louder and louder as their blades clashed and the intensity began to build. Metatron was becoming impatient and decided it was time to push her as far as he could.

'Metatron, ease up on him!' yelled Michael.

Metatron was fighting as hard as he could to the point where, as skillful a fighter as Gabriel was, even he was losing his step.

Berenike could feel the anxiety emerging in her as she watched the fight. She was worried for Gabriel. Metatron swung his sword at Gabriel and knocked him to the floor. When Metatron raised his blade above Gabriel to strike at him once again, Berenike screamed.

'No!'

As she ran towards Gabriel without a thought, she raised her hand, and as the brightest of lights shot out from her, it knocked Metatron flying across the room. Berenike's legs forced her to the floor. The light now encased her body from head to toe; it had now been brought to the surface.

Berenike crawled to Gabriel on her hands and knees. 'That's my girl,' he said under his breath, holding out his arms to her.

'Are you OK, Gabe?' Berenike trembled as Gabriel held her.

'Of course.' He giggled to himself as he held her tight. They were both about to stand up when Gabriel took a closer look at her. 'You're glowing, Berenike.'

Michael and Raphael both helped Metatron up from the ground. Although shocked, Michael knew exactly what Metatron was thinking. The intensity from the light surrounding her made them squint. Next to God's light, it was the brightest light they'd ever seen, including the light from the Morningstar, Jovan.

'Well, now that we know she has it, let's make sure she knows how to use it,' said Uriel.

'Metatron and Uriel will oversee your training,' said Michael.

'So that's why he wants me. You said he could use my light to destroy God's Kingdom. I'm a weapon.'

'Berenike, we have never encountered a being like you before. Your abilities are new to us as well,' Michael tried to reassure her as her anxiety was building.

'Will he kill me, Michael?' she asked.

Michael embraced his daughter. He was just as scared for her as she was for herself. 'I will die before I let him harm one hair on your head!'

Berenike was now convinced he was hiding something from her. She knew he was keeping secrets, as Michael was being extremely protective of her.

'It's time you told me everything, Michael.' She threw her sword on the floor as she left the combat room. Berenike was feeling a mix of anger, fear and betrayal. She needed answers, especially from Michael. 'You deceived me, Michael. You tricked me to see if I'd use that thing inside me.' Berenike was confused. 'No more secrets, do you hear me?' Just as Gabriel and the others caught up with them, Berenike finally asked the question they all knew was coming. 'Who am I?'

'You are a child of God's light.' Michael was nervous as he struggled to speak.

'Yes, I know I'm a child of God's light, everyone keeps saying that - but I'm also part mortal, as my mother was human!'

'That's right. Part High Priestess, actually.'

'So, I'm part human, part ...' Michael remained silent while Berenike's frustration was on the boil. 'How do you all know so much about my family?' she asked, directing the question to Gabriel. 'What aren't you telling me? I'm going to ask you one more time, Michael. Tell me who am I!' she demanded as she confronted him.

'What happens if I don't tell you?' Michael knew he couldn't keep teasing her for long.

'Then I'll leave!' she said defiantly.

'Where are you going to run to?' Michael could not help grinning. He could see the stubborn little girl within her still. 'There's nowhere you can go. I'll find you no matter where you are.'

Michael was now smiling at her as the others looked on in amusement. Berenike took a deep breath, as she was almost at the brink of tears.

He raised his hand to touch her cheek. Everyone in the room could feel the emotions coming from both father and daughter. He trembled as he spoke.

'You're part human, but mostly Archangel. You're my daughter.'

Berenike froze. A feeling of confusion swept over her. 'But you abandoned me. You didn't want me. You sent me away!'

Michael took a step back from her in shock. He felt guilty enough as it was, but to hear the words from his own child was more than he could bear.

Metatron pushed Raphael forward as he stumbled into the

conversation. 'Child, it wasn't Michael's choice to let you go; it was God's command,' said Raphael.

'A lot happened on the day God banished Jovan. You were sent away to protect you. We were in fear of what you would become, and God knew Jovan would come for you. It was the day your mother died, and the day Jovan and the others rebelled against our Kingdom - which, incidentally, you've now become its protector. It is your birthright. I can tell you, it was the worst day your father has ever lived. None of us will ever forget that day. He lost your mother and you both on the same day.'

'I was with him when he found your mother. She died in his arms. It broke his heart, dear one. We all felt his pain...we still do,' said Gabriel.

Michael had left the others to talk to Berenike while he walked back to the balcony. He felt a sense of peace in the rays of the light they'd both observed earlier together. He stood there, allowing the rays to heal his pain as the light of his creator touched his face.

'Father, help her forgive me,' he said as he looked out into the horizon of the Heavens.

'He loves you,' said Raphael, 'maybe remember that when you get angry with him, child.' Raphael bowed his head as he left her to absorb the information they'd shared.

The Archangels, including Gabriel, all wanted Berenike to think about the sacrifice Michael had made at the cost of his heart.

Berenike walked out to the balcony where Michael was standing. She didn't know what to say to him. As they stood side by side, she placed her hand on his. As she faced her father, as well as her anger, she could see the tears welling in his eyes as his emotions began to overflow. Michael wept in his child's arms as he looked for forgiveness. As she held him, she was overwhelmed with compassion for him.

As Michael stood there holding his daughter, he felt a mix of emotions as they quietly spoke to each other.

'This place is a big adjustment,' she stated.

'I'll help you with that,' Michael said enthusiastically. 'Your mind must be racing.'

Berenike nodded in agreement. 'I'm sorry I got mad at you. Raphael told me you weren't the one who sent me away. I have a few things to say to your employer about that too!' Berenike watched her father smiling back at her. His love for her was shining bright. 'Did you mean it when you said you wouldn't let Jovan hurt me?'

Michael tenderly stroked her hair. 'Of course. Why would you say that?'

'When I hit Metatron with the light, I could feel it rising within me. I wasn't sure if I'd be able to control it. That light is like nothing I've ever felt before. If I hadn't been so exhausted, I don't think I would have stopped. What if next time I'm not able to stop it? What if I hurt you or Gabe or any of the others?'

'We're all here to help you. You'll learn to control it,' he reassured her. 'You know, being part Archangel, you will have special gifts. You'll learn how to use them.'

'I feel like I've walked into a fantasy world.'

'Berenike, it's as real as your life on Earth. You are going to have to learn to defend yourself, and quickly. I want you to work with Metatron, Uriel, and Raphael on your training as I said before, and of course, Gabriel and I will be here for you. You have become quite fond of him, haven't you?'

Berenike blushed as she nodded. 'He likes to talk, and he's very kind.' Her father watched her. She was trying to hide how much she liked him, but she was failing. 'What if I can't control it, Michael?'

'Michael!?' He frowned.

'Father.' She smiled. 'I've never called anyone that before.' She hugged him as tightly as she could.

Michael couldn't wipe the smile from his face. 'I'm sorry you must carry this burden on your shoulders. Doesn't seem fair. Why don't you go and get some rest. You've had a huge day.'

She nodded in agreement.

'Don't go too far, OK?' Michael said, still holding her hand.

'I'll be close by.'

Michael kissed his child goodnight, and Berenike went to lie down. She closed her eyes, exhausted from the day and its events.

CHAPTER SEVEN

PROPHECY AND VISION

A few hours later, Michael crept into Berenike's room to watch her sleep, something he hadn't done since she was a baby. She quietly slept as he smiled at his little girl, playing with the curl of her hair that fell into her face.

Michael had fallen asleep in the chair beside her bed. He stirred as he heard his daughter's distress, waking, startled, as Uriel rushed into the room.

'What's wrong?'

'I thought it was a dream, but I think she's having a vision. Whatever it is she's seeing, it's distressing her.'

Michael reached out to touch her. 'No, do not touch her; just let it play out.' Uriel's eyes shaded over white as the light shone from him.

'Can you see what she's seeing?'

'Almost.' The look on Uriel's face was frightening. Being an

Angel of prophecy and vision, he could see and feel exactly what Berenike was experiencing in her visions.

'I've seen enough. Come, Michael.'

They left and joined the Archangels in the seventh level of Heaven with God. What he'd just seen in Berenike's vision had to be shared. They needed to prepare for what was to come.

'Sleep,' Michael said as he touched her forehead.

Just as Michael commanded, Berenike slipped into a deep slumber.

The Archangels regrouped in the Holy Court before God, and Uriel began to share with his fellow Archangels what he'd just seen in Berenike's vision. Nervous, Uriel's eyes shaded over white and his body beamed the crystal white light of the creator.

'What did she see, Uriel?' Michael asked.

'Great darkness. Jovan's control of the underworld is strong. He has many sympathisers, but he's being directed like a puppet. He has someone controlling him. He will come for her, but I can tell you, she's strong enough to defeat him. I am sure of that. The people of Earth, on the other hand, are about to go through great trials.'

'What do you mean?' Gabriel asked. He was concerned, as were the others.

'They have the fight of their lives ahead of them. On both sides, many will perish as Jovan brings the fight to the surface. There will be darkness like they've never seen before. He will bring his army to the surface, and they will all have to fight. Humanity will stand side by side with us and form an alliance as they are drawn out onto the streets. Every beast imaginable will surface before them.'

'My lord, our records refer to this as the Apocalypse,' said Metatron to God.

'I don't feel it's the same one,' said Uriel. 'There will be two large battles. There will be great destruction as day becomes night. They will cower down like scared animals before him. The loss of life on both sides will be extreme. Unless we stop him.' Uriel took a deep breath.

'All guardians need to be put on alert immediately,' said God. Each Archangel knew with God addressing them on the situation, the matter was becoming serious.

God stood up from his throne and left the room. Michael could see the worry etched on God's face as he followed him, leaving his fellow Archangels in the throne room. God paced the floor as Michael entered the room.

'It will happen again, Michael. I knew this day would come.'

'Lord, this is not your fault. You of all know how unstable Jovan is. No matter how much you gave him, he always wanted more. He's a spoilt child.'

'Your anger toward him is understandable, Michael, but he is my child. I have a feeling I will have to step in again to save humanity from him.'

Michael had never seen God so worried. Sending Jovan away and banishing him from His Kingdom had broken God's heart.

'You've forgotten something, my Lord. We have Berenike.'

'Will she be ready, Michael?'

'Yes, my Lord, she will be ready. She will stand side by side with us in defence of the Heavens.' Michael knew somehow the fate of eternity was in his daughter's hands and it was connected to Jovan.

As they all left, Gabriel wanted answers from Uriel.

'Uriel, I know you're not telling us everything. What else did you see?'

Uriel was hesitant. Gabriel would be persistent until he had answers.

'When the time comes, she will need you.' Uriel's eyes shaded over. 'Unfortunately, what you are about to go through with her, none of us can prepare you for. Stand strong, my friend, and don't give up hope where she is concerned.'

Gabriel wasn't sure what to make of his comments. As Uriel left the room, he spoke the words that would stay with Gabriel forever.

'Gabriel, you will mean more to her than even she can comprehend right now. She will love you as much as you love her. That's all I can share with you for now.'

Uriel smiled as he left the throne room.

CHAPTER EIGHT

THE GIFT

Berenike woke from a restful sleep and glanced over at the chair that sat beside her bed. Draped over it was a gold dress made of silk. It was the most beautiful dress she'd ever seen. She placed the dress over her head, and as the length of the garment fell to the floor, she stood in front of the mirror. The bodice section of the dress fit her snugly. The neckline was tall and shaped and curved up into her neck. She looked like a princess. She was now part of the Royal Family of Heaven. She could see how different she was now.

It was quiet outside the palace, the perfect time to explore. As Berenike left her room, she could see Gabriel hovering nervously outside her doorway. He brought a smile to her face. As he watched her approach, she was breathtaking. She looked beautiful. As his heart skipped a beat, he welcomed her with a smile.

'Are you rested, dear one?'

'Yes. Do you like my dress? I found it in my room. I have no idea who left it there, but someone has very good taste.'

She preened and fidgeted and spun around, displaying her new gown until the dress sat comfortably on her skin.

'I took a guess on your size,' Gabriel was extremely shy as he explained. He was hoping she liked it. 'I had the tailor down in the city make it for me to give to you.'

'Gabe, thank you. It's beautiful. I've never worn anything like this before.' He was happy she was so impressed with his gift.

'So, how much of Heaven have you seen?' Gabriel knew she'd only briefly viewed her surroundings and was eager to show her Heaven.

'Not much. I took the tour on my own.'

'May I show you?' he said as he held out his hand.

'I'd like that.' As she took his hand, Gabriel noticed she was very uneasy.

'Are you all right, dear one?'

'I had a bad dream,' she said, confused.

Berenike looked worried. Gabriel knew the vision she just received had shaken her to the core, as it did Uriel.

'I guess I didn't expect to dream in Heaven. It's hard to know what's normal here and what isn't.'

'Well, this will cheer you up.'

'Promise?'

'Yes, I promise.' He smiled.

Gabriel held her hand and escorted her from the palace down into the city. As they walked down the main street, people were smiling and running from door to door with excitement. It was a rare occasion that an Archangel would take a walk through the city. They were all very excited.

Berenike could see an old woman was trying to catch up to her. As she stopped to face her, she reached out her hand.

'Bless you, friend,' she said to the woman.

Gabriel smiled. 'Berenike, I'd like you to meet Maggie. She made your dress.'

Berenike was overwhelmed by the gesture. She hugged her. The sound of gasping from the crowd of people could be heard through several streets of the city.

'Oh Maggie, thank you, it's beautiful. I love it.'

Gabriel reached for her hand and gave it a comforting squeeze as they continued to walk towards the end of the street. She felt like a rock star. She hadn't expected to be on display but welcomed the attention and warmth from the souls in the city.

Gabriel led Berenike into the gardens and over the Rainbow Bridge. She stopped and looked back at the Heavenly Palace; just the sight of it took her breath away. The building itself was white with Gothic-like steeples. The architecture in Heaven was magnificent, as the buildings reached high into the sky. They resembled some very familiar churches and buildings from Earth and were extremely white. As her eyes met with the top of the building, she could see the golden beams of light from the top level of the palace. The Seventh Heaven.

'Is that where He is, Gabriel?'

'Yes. If you look carefully, the throne room is on the very top level. It's where the gold light is.' Gabriel pointed to the top of the palace.

'It's so beautiful.'

Gabriel watched her. It was like looking at something for the first time. He was seeing his surroundings through fresh eyes. Her eyes. The palace had never shone brighter or looked more beautiful.

'I thought the gardens would be of interest to you.'

'You know me too well.'

'Yes, I do.'

'The colours are amazing. We don't have anything like this on Earth.'

'Of course not; this is Heaven.' Gabriel was full of pride.

'Gabe, why do I look so different now?'

'What do you mean, dear one?'

'Well, I look better. This is so embarrassing,' she gushed.

Gabriel laughed. 'When you return home to Heaven, your spirit returns to its original form. Your original form and appearance. This is how you were always meant to be seen. I guess the easiest way to answer your question is to say Heaven suits you.' Gabriel could be very intense at times when it came down to his feelings for her. 'You would be beautiful to me in any form, dear one.'

She smiled at his affection for her. 'I'll remind you you said that when I'm old and wrinkly.'

They both laughed.

'Berenike, you do understand you are one of the immortals now. You are one of us. You won't grow old, dear one. You will remain in this form.'

For a moment, she thought about what he said. 'No, I didn't know that. You make it sound so serious, Gabriel.'

'It's God's gift to us as his Angels.' He smiled. 'Immortality is a blessing not all beings get to experience.'

Gabriel continued to pick several flowers from the ground around them, choosing the ones with the strongest fragrance for her as he created a bouquet of colour. As he handed them to her, the blush of Berenike's cheeks became as vibrant as her smile.

'Thank you,' she said shyly as she accepted them from him. Berenike's

They continuously chatted and laughed, enjoying each other's company. They played in the field like children and walked hand in hand through the gardens as Gabriel showed her the Heaven he loved, the same Heaven she would grow to love as well. They talked about everything and anything and giggled at each other's remarks like teenagers. Berenike was immersing herself into Gabriel's soul, and to her, he was touching her heart in ways no man before him had ever done. Gabriel held on to her every word as they chatted about her life on Earth.

In the distance, Michael was watching his daughter and his friend. It brought back memories of the time he'd spent with her mother. Michael could now see what Uriel had observed earlier, and the smile disappeared from his face. It was very clear to him his friend and daughter had developed a strong bond.

Uriel and Michael stood side by side, watching them. As they stood in silence, they observed Berenike and Gabriel smile and laugh as he escorted her through the gardens.

'Gabriel is in love with her, isn't he?' Michael asked.

'Yes, Michael, he is,' Uriel said hesitantly.

'Will you keep an eye on her for me?'

Uriel nodded, then Michael left the room, saying nothing.

'Gabriel, Father said you've been with me for a long time. Thank you for not leaving my side,' Berenike said.

Gabriel smiled as he stood close to her.

'And I never will.' He placed a flower in her hair. 'Come, dear one. I'll walk you back.'

As they arrived back at her room, still holding hands, Gabriel wasn't letting go.

Berenike stood on her toes to kiss him on the cheek. 'Thank you, Gabe. I had a really nice time with you. Thank you again for the dress.'

She smiled as Gabriel leaned in to kiss her. As Berenike was about to experience one of the most romantic moments of her life, Michael appeared.

'Gabriel, we have a meeting. Come,' he said. Gabriel nodded. 'Berenike, I have a few things to do, and then we can spend some time together,' said Michael.

'OK.'

As they left, she caught Gabriel's eye and smiled. Her heart was racing with excitement as he disappeared with her father.

CHAPTER NINE

NEW FRIENDS

Left to her own devices, Berenike decided it was time she started tapping in to her gifts, especially since everyone was eager to see how she would develop her special abilities. Michael had told her as an Archangel, she was special, but they had no idea what to expect from her, as she was a unique being of light.

As she stood on her bedroom balcony, Berenike took a deep breath and closed her eyes. She thought of what she wanted to appear before her. She could feel the power building within her, from her toes to the top of her head, as she conjured a sword. It was a small blade with a thick handle. Nothing overtly impressive, but it had been more important to her that she was able to manifest it.

Raphael entered her room and watched her manifest through her thoughts. He was quite impressed.

'Who taught you to do that, child?'

'Father told me all I had to do was think of what I wanted and then let it manifest.'

'You're grasping this all very quickly, but I do believe you knew you had it in you anyway. You just forgot being human.' He smiled at her as he instantly put her at ease.

'Raph, it's strange; it's not until you're here in this place that you realise you really do have that power within you. It's like unlocking a door.'

He watched her conjure several other small items, such as flowers and even shooting stars. She could move different objects with her light. As she took on all the challenges Raphael gave her, she couldn't help noticing the change in his demeanour.

'Is something wrong, Raph?' she asked.

'Everything is fine, child. I was just thinking about how good it is to have you with us, finally. Your father is very happy you're here. We all are. We've been waiting a long time for your arrival.' He sighed as his expression changed. 'You know, we all agreed it was wrong to send you away. We never wanted you to go.' Berenike stood in silence, listening to what he had to say. 'No matter how frightening it was at the time to have you in our world, we never would have wished that upon Michael.' For a moment, she could see the regret within his eyes. 'You've certainly brought a little excitement to the place, especially down in the city, not to mention the palace as well.'

She smiled. 'Can I go and visit them down in the city?'

'Of course you can. They would all love to see you again, and I think it would be good for you to make some friends. I know you miss your friends back on Earth.'

'Terribly. As beautiful as this place is, Raph, and as much as I love the fact that I'm now with Father and the rest of you, I still miss it.' She looked out into the horizon from her balcony. 'It's as if I'm mourning my life, but at the same time I feel like I've come home. I can't explain it.'

'Many feel like that, Berenike. The transition to a spiritual life here is a hard adjustment at times because of the life you led on Earth. Human beings become so used to the fact that they only see what is in front of them in the third dimension. The idea of another type of existence, well, it is foreign to them. Some souls on Earth do have insight into our world; once they arrive, their transition is easier. But for others, it can take a while. That will not be the case for you though. Look at you. You have learnt so much already just by tapping in to your own connection with the light. We're all very proud of you.' Raphael was enjoying his time with her.

'You know...' She hesitated. 'You're pretty cool for an Archangel, Raph.'

'I know,' he said proudly.

Berenike giggled as she gave him a hug. She quite liked Raphael. He was very normal. She kissed his cheek, and he blushed.

Uriel entered her room to join them and took the blade from her. 'Nice blade.' She was nervous around Uriel. His powerful presence made her quite jittery.

'Does anyone here know how to knock?' Berenike snapped.

Raphael and Uriel stared at each other blankly, not fully understanding the comment. She frowned. Metatron decided he would join them as well.

'OK, so why don't you test out your sword, child?' asked Metatron.

Berenike swung her sword. As she skillfully demonstrated what she'd learnt so far, all three Archangels went into a full attack formation against her. Berenike fought hard, knocking them to the ground.

As her sword fell out of her hand, the beams of light that were within her formed to defend her as she knocked Uriel from one side of the room to the other, flat on his back.

'Uriel, I'm so sorry.' She apologised repeatedly.

Uriel got up and walked out of the room. She noticed Michael and Gabriel had quietly joined them.

'I think you bruised his ego, dear one.' Gabriel couldn't help laughing.

'You said I'd be able to control it. You said I wouldn't hurt anyone,' she yelled at Michael as she ran out of the room.

Gabriel was about to go after her when Michael stopped him.

'It's between Uriel and Berenike. He should be the one to go after her,' said Michael.

Berenike ran out of the room in tears. Her biggest fear was that the light within her would hurt one of the Archangels, and her fears had now manifested into reality.

As Uriel searched for Berenike throughout Heaven, he found Berenike in the gardens sobbing.

'Berenike, please stop crying. I'm fine, see? No damage.' Uriel patted his chest as he sat down next to her.

'I'm sorry,' she cried.

He could see the child in her, and his heart softened at the sight of her tears.

'Uriel, it's getting stronger,' Berenike said.

'Good, that's what we want. I'm actually happy you whipped my butt.' He grinned as she laughed in-between her tears. 'No one's done that in quite a while. I'm enjoying the challenge. The more you bring it to the surface and use it, the easier it will be to control the power within you. Do not be afraid of it. Do not be afraid of any of your gifts. You are the daughter of an Archangel. You're magnificent. Let your light shine.' He smiled. 'I wish you could see what I see in you.'

Berenike 's eyes widened as his statement took her by surprise. Uriel's eyes then shaded white as he received a vision.

'You have a great deal ahead of you, and it's not going to be easy for you, but if I can leave you with anything, know that you are loved and protected more than you know. We are all here for you.'

She hadn't realised just how much her fear had clouded her judgment towards him. He wasn't so harsh after all. She had the completely wrong impression of him.

As Berenike walked through the gardens, she received comfort from the beauty and scent of her surroundings. She could see other Angels with their wings spread wide, basking in the rays of Heaven once again. She saw several Angels launch themselves into the air and fly. The light at one point blinded her sight, and she raised her hand in front of her eyes and began to run. She chased the Angels along the path out of the gardens and back again, laughing as they laughed with her.

'Well, if they can fly, then I must be able to as well. 'Don't be frightened of it,' he says. OK, here we go.'

She closed her eyes and began to float higher and higher as she took flight into the light.

Michael was in the Seventh Heaven with Gabriel when he spoke.

'Michael, come quickly. You need to see this.' They both stood side by side, watching Berenike.

'She's learning quickly.' Michael was proud of her.

'That is quite possibly the most beautiful thing I have ever seen.' Gabriel smiled to himself. 'That's my girl,' he whispered.

Uriel was still on his way back to the Holy Palace when he looked up into the sky. He stood there smiling at Berenike as she flew higher and higher into the light, then suddenly smiled to himself as he realised his pep talk had worked wonders.

'Well done, Berenike.'

Berenike was floating in the Heavens, radiating the light of God. She was shining like a beacon. The other Angels surrounding her were rejoicing in the light rays with her, and she opened her eyes to see them dancing and singing in front of her.

The energy radiating through her body filled her with strength. She felt alive as the source of all life moved throughout her body and soul. As word spread that she was the light child and Michael was her father, the beings of Heaven all surrounded her to unify as one. She began to feel a connection to all the celestial beings that were presenting themselves to her.

After Berenike's walk through the city, many wanted to meet her. Several Angels plucked up the courage to say hello to her, and as they took her hand, they guided her closer to the light. Berenike could feel her body being charged full of energy, enjoying the warmth from the light she could feel from her father beside her once again.

Michael whispered in her ear, 'It's not like sunbaking, Berenike. You can come back, you know. As many times as you like, in fact.'

Berenike laughed as she opened one eye at her father. 'That's very funny, an Archangel with a sense of humour. Imagine that!' She laughed.

'Father, why don't I have wings?' she asked, looking around at the other Angels.

Michael had to think for a moment. It was a good question.

'Honestly, I don't know, Berenike. More than likely because you're part human, and I'd say your human side was more dominant than your angelic side when you were born.'

'I wish I had wings like yours,' she said.

'In case you haven't noticed, you don't seem to need them,' he declared to his daughter.

'OK.'

Michael laughed. 'Let's go,' he said, taking her hand. 'I want to take you somewhere. I have something to show you.'

Intrigued, she agreed.

CHAPTER TEN

MICHAEL'S PLACE

Michael was aching to spend more time with his daughter.

'Where are we going, Father?' Berenike asked.

'This is where I feel closest to your mother.'

Michael had taken Berenike to a very special place. It was a small garden with lush grass and room enough for the two of them.

'Here, sit down with me,' he said as they sat on the grass. 'I buried your mother here, so many years ago.' Michael had brought Berenike to the most important place on Earth. To him, this was where he would come to feel closer to the woman he loved.

'I see how much you miss her, Father. I guess I'm a reminder of her. That must be hard for you?' Berenike said.

'You're the most amazing reminder.' Michael leaned over and kissed her on the cheek.

'Is Mother really in here?' Berenike pointed to a section of grass they were sitting in front of.

'Just her body; her spirit is always with us back in Heaven.'

No sooner had she spoken, Berenike manifested a bunch of roses to place on top of the grave. 'It would be nice to give her these in person one day.'

'You really have that under control, don't you?'

Berenike was beginning to master her special gifts, and Michael was surprised at how quickly she was learning everything.

'Father, when do I get to see her? Doesn't she want to meet me?'

'I'm not sure, Berenike. I don't see her that much either. I do sense her at times though. That's my punishment for loving her. I guess for the moment I'll have to be enough for you.'

Berenike squeezed Michael's hand. 'That's fine with me. How many girls get to have an Archangel as their Father?' She gathered up the courage to ask him a question. 'Can I ask you something?'

'Of course you can.'

Michael was enjoying the conversation and small talk with her. He loved her curiosity. It gave him an opportunity to step proudly into the role that had eluded him for many centuries; the role of father.

'Did you ever love anyone besides Mother?' she asked timidly. 'I mean, I'm not sure how many women Archangels fall in love with, so I was just curious, I guess.'

Michael knew curiosity wasn't the reason she was asking. He took a deep breath and spoke from his heart. 'There was never anyone before and never anyone since your mother,' he said sadly. 'Archangels don't normally have relationships like you do on Earth, Berenike, but when we fall in love, we are bonded to that person for an eternity. When two hearts become bonded to each other, they burn as twin flames. It's not an easy journey at times, but the love is unbreakable, no matter how long it's for.' His comment made her think of Gabriel. 'Love is the strongest emotion in existence. Never doubt the love we give; it's God's gift to us.'

She realised he was right. 'It seems so simple. The way everybody thinks in Heaven is so uncomplicated. I never realised just how much human beings muck things up.'

As the days passed, Berenike realised she was becoming more and more of a spiritual being. The way human beings think could be easily influenced, and each experience gave her an insight into how humans think.

'You know, there's a saying back on Earth: love can change the world. Until humanity takes its place here, they'll never really understand what that means. Am I right?'

Michael placed his arm around his daughter's shoulder. 'You got it,' he said proudly.

As they sat enjoying their father and daughter moment, Berenike began to wonder about home. What was life like now back on Earth? Were her friends OK? How was the shop going?

'Father, I'd like to see Amy. Is that kind of thing allowed?'

'I think that would be OK. Just don't frighten her, all right?'

'All right,' she said as they sat there together, enjoying the peace.

'So how are you and Gabriel getting on? You've been spending a lot of time with him.' Michael was fishing for information. He faced his daughter, awaiting the answer to his question.

'Father, I'm going to go see Amy. I'll find you when I get back.' She kissed her father's cheek as she got up and disappeared.

'Just as I thought,' he said with a heavy sigh. He sat there quietly on his own, enjoying the peace and quiet. 'Sarra, our daughter's in love.'

'Yes, she is.' Sarra appeared and sat down next to Michael on the grass. 'As much as you want to control the situation, my love, you can't control a woman's heart, no matter how hard you try,' she said with a smile.

Michael put his arm around Sarra and kissed her cheek. 'I've missed you,' he said.

'I miss you too.' Sarra could hear a voice calling her. 'I have to go my love. Take care of our daughter; she's going to need her father with what's to come. I love you.'

Every time Michael saw her, he felt his heart rip in two, but not seeing her was worse. He would hold on to every moment with her.

Michael sat quietly as he thought of his family. At some point, he would have to explain to Berenike her duty to the Heavens. He knew her connection to Gabriel was strong. The father in him was emerging, and he knew he had to tread lightly where his daughter's heart was concerned.

CHAPTER ELEVEN

WARNINGS

Several months had passed with Amy becoming the sole beneficiary of Berenike's Last Will and Testament. She'd left the business, her house, and all her material possessions to her best friend. Amy and EJ decided it was time to start sorting out the house into some form of order so Amy could move on from the loss of her friend. Muffin had also become her pet. With all the furniture covered in sheets, it was time to unveil the remnants of her dear friend.

It had been several months since Berenike had passed away and returned home, and EJ and Amy missed her terribly. Muffin sat there watching them pack and reorganise boxes for storage. Muffin could not only sense her, she could also see Berenike, and she began to bark out of control at her. Amy wasn't sure what was going on. She stood there in front of Muffin, confused, as she watched Muffin specifically barking toward the lounge room.

'What on Earth are you barking at, dog?' she yelled as she stood there staring.

Suddenly, Berenike began to reveal herself to her friends. Amy stood there, shocked, unable to speak. EJ entered the room and could see Berenike as clear as day. *Smash!* The cup EJ was holding plummeted to the floor as he saw Berenike before him.

'Hello.'

Amy moved closer to her friend and reached out her hand to touch Berenike. 'Oh my god...it's really you.'

Tears welled in Amy's eyes. As they embraced each other, their tears and laughter were overflowing. EJ was shocked, and as he hugged his friend, the emotion of the situation overwhelmed him and he cried. Berenike looked down at Muffin, who was sitting, wagging her tail.

'How are you, little one?' Berenike asked Muffin, who barked back. Berenike picked her up, then hugged and kissed her pet, who she'd missed so much. 'I've missed you so much, my little one,' she said as she cuddled Muffin.

'You look so different,' said EJ as he poked at Berenike to see if she was real.

Amy examined her friend from head to toe. 'You look beautiful.'

'I have so much to tell you both,' Berenike said.

'I'm so sorry I left you that night,' said Amy.

'Amy, that wasn't your fault. I slipped on the floor rug and hit my head as I fell. I drank way too much because of the visions I was having. None of this is your fault. Actually, it was just a matter of time.'

'Why are you here?'

'Well, I wanted to see you, and I need to warn you both.'

'Warn us? What on Earth are you talking about?'

Berenike stood up and paced the floor. 'OK, Cliff's Notes version. I am the child of an Archangel, and I possess the light of God. A fallen Angel wants to use my light as a weapon to kill God and take over Heaven. If he succeeds, life as we know it is over.'

EJ stood up and looked over at Amy, who burst into a fit of laughter. Berenike and EJ stood there quietly until Amy stopped laughing.

'Wow, you must have an endless supply of champagne up there, huh?' she said to her friend, who was completely stunned at her revelation.

'Amy, I'm not kidding,' Berenike said.

Still, Amy couldn't help laughing.

'He's coming after you?' asked EJ. Berenike nodded. 'What do you mean he wants your light?'

'Let me show you. Apparently, I've had this inside me my entire life. I'm still learning, but let me give it a go.' Berenike raised her hand and aimed for the lamp across the room. *Bang!* The beam of light burst out of her, shot across the room, and destroyed the lamp sitting on the edge of the table.

'I didn't like that lamp much anyway,' she said.

'I gave you that,' Amy snapped, her face screwed up with annoyance at her friend's destructive power.

'Oh.' Berenike quickly changed the subject as EJ grinned. 'When the time comes, you'll need to fight and defend each other.'

'How do you know all of this?' asked Amy.

'Remember the dreams I was having? Well, they were visions of the future. It *will* happen, Amy, and you need to be aware that you'll have the fight of your life ahead of you.'

No sooner had Berenike finished what she was saying, Michael appeared before them. 'I think you've said enough,' he said.

'Why can't I warn my friends? They deserve a fighting chance.' Berenike was angry.

'It's time to go.' Michael was being very stern with her.

'Who are you?' Amy stood forward to protect her friend. She was still protective of Berenike, even if she was dead.

'Amy, EJ, this is my father. His name is Michael.'

'Hang on a minute,' said EJ. 'If you're the daughter of an Archangel and your name is Michael,' he said, pointing to Michael. 'Then you're not?'

'Um, yep, that would be him.'

Berenike smiled as Michael frowned. His newfound celebrity status from her friends wasn't something he was enjoying, although Berenike was.

She giggled. 'Wait till you meet the others, EJ; it'll blow your mind. I have to go,' she said to her friends, 'but I'll see you again soon, OK? Amy, thank you for what you did at the funeral. It meant a lot to me, my friend.' She smiled at her friends and kissed them goodbye. 'Be brave, little Muffin,' Berenike said as she patted Muffin on the head, then said goodbye and disappeared in front of them.

'There's something we need to do,' said Michael. 'Let's go.'

As Gaige sat on the floor of his apartment, he raised his glass. The guilt of Berenike's passing was overwhelming. He'd been her protector through many lifetimes, but like Berenike, most of his past life memories had vanished through each passage of time. Now, they were coming back to him quickly. He threw the glass against the wall, and it smashed and crumbled into pieces as it slid to the bottom of the wall.

'I failed you,' he said as he looked over at a photograph of the two of them together. 'It's what I do best.'

He lifted the whiskey bottle to his mouth and tried desperately to dull the pain. The more he drank, the quicker he relived the memories of his past lives. Gaige was a warrior of God's Kingdom. As he started each new life with Berenike, his memories of each experience were scattered to the back of his mind. Gaige put his hands to his head, fists clenched. Tears began to fall.

Berenike sat down on the floor with him, observing him, noticing the pain in his eyes.

'Father, what's wrong with him? I've never seen him like this.' Berenike's concern for Gaige was genuine.

'Just as your memories will return, he's remembering his past lives with you. He's feeling your loss, Berenike. He's grieving.'

'But he didn't want me. He didn't care.'

'Berenike, no matter what the result was between you both, he did love you. It wasn't that he didn't want you; he was supposed to protect you on my command. He was conflicted with his duty to me and what he felt for you. He knew it was forbidden. I have to go. Stay with him for a while.'

Berenike nodded at her father's request. She was struggling with how she felt; she still felt hurt and resentment towards him. As they sat on the floor together, he could calm his thoughts, then he got up off the floor and proceeded to his bedroom to lie down and try to get some sleep.

As he lay in bed, Berenike wiped the tears from his eyes, then materialised before him.

'You?'

'What?' she asked.

'Oh, I'm going nuts for sure.' Gaige was sure he was hallucinating.

'You can see me? You're not supposed to see me unless I let you. That's how it works, I think.' Berenike sat up in the bed on her knees to talk to him.

'You're dead.'

'Yes, I know I'm dead.'

'You're talking to me; I'm definitely going insane.'

Gaige ran out of the room. As he slammed the door behind him,

Berenike was left completely stunned by the conversation she'd just had with him.

He can see me, she thought. 'Gaige, come back.'

She leapt up off the bed and ran towards the door. As she reached for the door handle, her body moved completely through the door and she fell flat on her face.

'Ouch!' she yelled. Gaige slowly moved closer towards her, not sure what to make of the situation. 'They didn't tell me I could move through things.'

Gaige could see how frustrated she was. 'Yeah, how about that.'

He reached out to help her up off the floor. 'It's OK. I can get up,' she said.

'Maybe you should sit down instead.'

He directed her to the lounge. As they sat side by side, he looked her over as if he was seeing her for the first time. As he sat silently with her, he plucked up the courage to speak.

'I don't understand this,' Gaige said. 'You died; I even went to your funeral. You're supposed to be reborn again, aren't you?'

'Not this time, I'm not. I saw you at the funeral. Oh, I'm sorry Amy slapped you.'

'You saw that?'

'Yeah, that girl's got a mean left hook.' Berenike giggled.

'So, you're an angel now?'

'No.'

'Really? You're a ghost, then?' he said as she laughed.

'I'm not really sure what I am. I'm not like the others.'

'Others?'

'Yes, the others in Heaven. I think I'm more Archangel, just without the wings.' Berenike got up off the lounge and walked over to the computer desk, where Gaige had placed a photo of Berenike and himself in a frame. 'You kept it.' She was quite surprised. 'They were good times, weren't they?'

'Yes, they were,' he said with a smile. 'I did care for you, Berenike.'

'Just not enough, right? You cared for you more.'

'Berenike, it was forbidden.'

'That didn't stop you!'

She was angry with him. She sat in silence with him as she felt a sense of sadness set in.

She sighed. 'There's so much I miss,' she said as she picked up the TV remote control and began to change the channels. Gaige took the remote control out of her hands and turned the TV off.

'Why don't we go for a walk like we used to?' he said.

Berenike smiled back at Gaige. It had been quite a while since he made her smile.

'We could take a walk along the beach if you want.' Gaige had remembered her favourite thing to do.

'I can't believe you remembered that. Thank you. I'd like that very much.' Her voice softened toward him. 'I'll meet you down there.'

Gaige jumped in his car and headed for the sunset strip. It was early in the morning, so the sun would be shining down, and it was Berenike's favourite time of the day. Gaige leaped out of the car and ran towards the water. He 'd been walking for about 15 minutes when he finally stopped. His eyes scanned the beach to find her.

'Looking for me?' she said, appearing before him.

'Come on, there's a nice spot up further I want to show you,' he said.

Berenike stood by the edge of the water with her eyes closed, breathing in the air. She opened her eyes to find Gaige staring back at her. Her hair was flowing in the breeze. Her eyes were bright, and she was glowing. To Gaige, she'd never looked more beautiful than she did in that moment.

'You have a glow about you.' Gaige raised his hand to her body to try to feel the energy radiating off her; it was warm.

'I know who I am now, Gaige. I am the daughter of Archangel Michael. He is my father. I am born of God's light.'

Gaige was shocked as it all fell into place. He had no idea she was Michael's daughter, but it all began to make sense the more he remembered.

'I wish I could change things,' he whispered.

'No,' she said, 'this was meant to happen. I know that now.'

Berenike raised her hand to touch his. 'Everything feels different, every touch, every breath. I never dreamt it would be like this. What awaits us after death is beautiful.'

They walked further along the beach, chatting about what had been happening to her.

'It's amazing, you know. There's a whole other world beyond what you see here out there. It's home, and here is where we learn lessons to expand our souls. To learn who we are as human beings.'

Gaige smiled. 'You know, I used to resent being here on Earth, but not once did I ever resent being with you.'

Berenike smiled at him, then bent down to immerse her hands in the ocean, cupped her hand, and scooped up a handful of water. As she poured the water into the palm of his hand, they both smiled.

'Can you feel it? Can you feel the water?' Berenike waited for his answer.

'What do you mean?'

'I can feel it...it's like I can feel the life force within it. I can feel everything. It's a little hard to explain, but it's like feeling beyond what you can see. It's a knowing. I mean, take the sun, for instance. When you watch a sunrise first thing in the morning and feel the sunlight on your face, well, I can feel the sun completely. I can feel its heat, its life force, and its true essence.' She closed her eyes. 'It's like you can feel where everything begins.'

'So, have you seen God?'

'No, but I know he's there, watching.'

Gaige couldn't help grinning at her comment as he could hear the annoyance in the tone of her voice.

'I have a strong feeling something bad is going to happen, Gaige. There's a bad guy on his way, and he's either going to kill me or use me to take down the Kingdom. He'll bring me in front of God's throne. I've seen it in a vision I had.'

'What are you talking about?' Gaige was concerned.

'He's what's been referred to as a fallen Angel. He wants to take over the Heavens and rule in place of God. His lust for power consumed him many years ago. He's done some terrible things, and now he wants me to complete his takeover.'

'You mean Jovan?' he asked. 'I was there the first time he tried to take God's throne.'

'What did you just say?'

Gaige's memories were scattered. 'I'm only remembering little pieces of it all because it was a long time ago now,' he said to her. 'I've seen him. The visions started several months ago. Just before you died. I'd been having them on and off for a while but just put it down to bad dreams. They were always the same dreams, which I thought was odd. I was always in them, and they were all from different times in history. You were there too. Though every dream has the same context, I'm protecting you. There was even one with angels in it.'

'Gaige, they weren't dreams. They were memories of past lives, and you'll remember more and more now that Berenike has returned to us.' Just as quickly as Michael had appeared, Gaige was on bended knee.

'Michael,' he said as he bowed his head to him. 'I failed you.'

'No, Gaige, you're remembering as you should. You have been through many lifetimes with Berenike. Her death isn't your fault,' he said as he looked over at his daughter.

Berenike rolled her eyes. It was't the first time Michael had commented on his daughter's consumption of alcohol.

'How much do you remember?' Michael was curious.

'I have all these memories, but they're not in place; they're all scattered. I remember the day you placed her in my arms and told me her mother had been killed and I was to protect her until it became time for us all to stand and fight, and a few past lives, but that's about it. Michael, you should have told me she was your daughter!' Gaige was angry at Michael.

'I'm not sure how much you will remember. I guess we'll take it one step at a time.'

'I have to leave you for a while and consult with the others. Now that we have Gaige back, this changes the game. Stay out of trouble,' Michael said protectively to Berenike.

Gaige held Berenike in his arms and kissed her goodbye. 'I'll see you soon.'

She squeezed herself out of his embrace. Michael could see how uncomfortable she was; it took her completely by surprise. Many things had changed, and although she cared for Gaige, she'd never forget the hurt he caused her with his infidelities. He may have been from the heavens, but he was more human than even

Gaige realised. She was no longer in love with him. Her feelings for him were now in the past; her heart was now with Gabriel.

As they both arrived back in Heaven, Michael was furious at what he'd just witnessed between the two of them.

'You will never touch her again. Do you hear me? You are her protector, not her lover.'

'It's a bit late to start playing father!' Gaige said angrily.

As Michael raised his hand and hit him, the Archangels were shocked at Michael's reaction. Gabriel gripped Michael's arm as he attempted a second punch. Michael's fathering instincts were kicking in, to everyone's surprise, including himself.

'Stop this now!' said Gabriel.

Michael left to compose himself and his anger, and Gabriel took the opportunity to deliver his own message to Gaige.

'Are you all right?'

'Yeah,' Gaige said as he wiped blood from his cheek.

'Good, because if you ever touch her again like that, I'll kill you myself.'

The seriousness of Gabriel's tone had Gaige watching his words; he'd just kissed the woman he loved. Gabriel's declaration had startled the Archangels. A lot had changed, but most of all, Gaige had been away for a long time. The constant battles through the millennia of time between Heaven and Hell had left the Archangels with a strong bond for each other after Jovan's betrayal.

'Well, if you think you two can stop fighting long enough to talk strategy, maybe we can defeat him,' said Raphael. 'When you're ready, I'll see you both in the combat room.'

CHAPTER THIRTEEN

JOVAN'S TRUTH

When Michael took Gaige back to Heaven, Berenike decided to go to the only place she felt comfortable: her house. Jovan could sense she was alone, and he began his journey to the surface. As he appeared before her, his stare was fierce as he looked her over from head to toe.

'You're not afraid of me?' he said to her as he paced the floor around her.

'No, are you going to hurt me?'

'I don't want to, but it is a possibility.' He grinned.

'Fight it!'

'Do you have any idea how long I've waited for you, Berenike?'

She rolled her eyes at him and took a deep breath. 'Maybe you should keep waiting, Jovan.'

'Feisty, aren't you? I like that.' He laughed.

Berenike stepped away from him. Due to her training, she knew she could match him, but she was still being cautious. His silent interrogation was intimidating.

Jovan smirked. 'I see they've told you stories about me?'

'No, just that you were a spoilt brat that fell from grace, and you murdered my mother,' Berenike said.

'That was truly an accident,' he said.

She could feel his demeanour change with his tone of voice. 'As the story goes, they say you threw it all away. Why?'

Jovan was surprised at her. He didn't expect that question to come from her, nor did he think she would listen.

'No one has ever bothered to ask me that question,' he said, genuinely surprised. 'It wasn't intentional.'

'Well, the floor's yours. Start talking.'

He examined her cold stare. She could feel herself being drawn to him. He was seductive in a way she'd never felt before.

'You human beings are so blessed,' he said angrily. 'My creator gave you free will. He permitted you to feel, to experience all life should offer. To create life. Although many of you take it for granted.'

She nodded. 'Well, I can't wrong you there,' she said. 'But that doesn't excuse the rest of what you did.'

'My creator and I didn't see eye-to-eye on many things. I wanted to experience the things his human race had. I loved humanity, as I was meant to, but I could not understand some of the things they did. They needed to be punished for what they had done wrong, for not following God's law. Your father was different. He understood what they were about. I used to joke with him that he was more human than Archangel at times.'

'Jovan, even human beings don't understand at the best of times why they do some of the things they do,' she said.

'I did not agree with how things were being conducted. Heaven could have been quite a different place if the Father had listened to me. Many of my angels felt the same way, so we decided to change things.'

'Your angels? I don't understand.'

'Yes, I was the leader of God's army. I had thought your father was ready to stand by my side, but I was wrong. We were good friends once, he and I. We were like brothers,' he stated with a smile.

'Oh, I'm sure you were - until you murdered the woman he loved.' At that point, Berenike was losing patience and she stood up to leave.

'With your help, we can right the wrong done to me.'

She stared at him in disbelief. 'The wrong done to you? You killed my mother!' Her instincts were telling her to be careful of his lies and seductions.

'I know it's a lot for you to take in. I will give you some time.'

As he stood closer to her, she was weakening to his seductions, and she could feel the fear rising within as she gradually weakened in his arms. Jovan was trying to seduce her. What he felt between them was overwhelming. It was different than what she'd felt with Gabriel. Jovan exuded lust. It was like poison to a being of light; whereas she could feel the love in Gabriel's heart, being near Jovan was literally making her sick.

Jovan released her from his grip, not sure what he was feeling. 'Will you answer a question for me?' he asked.

'All right,' she agreed.

'What does being in love feel like?'

Berenike realised he wasn't like the other Archangels. There was a sadness projecting from his words. Jovan had only experienced jealousy, envy, and lust; up until now, the experience of love had eluded him. She stood there for a moment, thinking about what love was to her - then she thought about Gabriel and smiled.

'Well, it's magical. Being in love is many different emotions, but when you find the right person and your soul recognises them, everything falls into place. You would sacrifice everything for them, do anything for them without hesitation. It's so many different emotions. Do you understand, Jovan?' He remained by her side, listening. 'No, I don't suppose you do,' she said.

Jovan looked Berenike in the eye as he quietly said, 'I am truly sorry about your mother. I must go now.'

Before he disappeared, he took one last look at her before returning to Hell. She felt he genuinely was sorry, and it was at that moment she could see there was an element of Archangel still residing within him. It was probably the first time in centuries he'd been honest.

Jovan returned to his dominion and sat straight back on his throne, completely unnerved by his encounter with Berenike. His counsel had returned.

'Sire,' said Minion.

'Go, leave me alone. Do not come until you are called!'

Jovan was full of anger. He sat on his throne, disturbed by what had just taken place with Berenike. The years had made him lonely. He was becoming restless. Berenike had reminded him of the life he so desperately wanted; a life he nearly toppled the Kingdom of God to attain.

Jovan wasn't the only one bothered by the conversation. Berenike sat down on the lounge just as Gabriel appeared.

'Are you all right?' asked Gabriel as he ran to her.

She threw her arms around him and said nothing. He held her tight. She was relieved to see him. 'Yes, I'm fine.'

'I sensed he was with you; I was worried I wouldn't get to you in time.'

Gabriel stroked her hair and looked her over to see if she was hurt.

'He was. Gabe, I need to ask you something.'

'Of course, dear one, anything,' he said, smiling at her.

'I need to know what happened in the lead up to Jovan trying to take the throne.'

The smile she'd so quickly placed on his face disappeared.

'Berenike, what do you mean? Exactly what is it you want to know?' Berenike sat stubbornly waiting for an answer. 'OK, well, we watched him slowly become more and more jealous of your father and mother. His desire for power and lust and greed were growing day by day. It was like standing back and watching a volcano erupt. Dear one, whatever he has said to you, it was just to make you feel sorry for him. Don't play into it.'

The Archangels appeared before them.

'I believe we have a chance to bring him back from evil. To redeem him,' she said enthusiastically.

'Are you crazy? said Raphael.

'Berenike, that's a beautiful thought, but he's too far gone,' said Michael.

'No, he's not, Father. I think you're wrong. I think you're all wrong. I think you've been living this way for so long, you can't see past your own resentment of him.'

Michael couldn't believe what he was hearing from his daughter. Berenike felt compassion for Jovan; however, she could still see the Archangel within him and knew it was fighting to get out.

'There is good still in him, Father. I've seen it. I think he can be saved.'

'Have you forgotten what he did, Berenike?'

Michael was still holding on to a lot of anger, as it had robbed him of being her father for many centuries. He wasn't human, but it was easy to see how humanity's behavioural traits had rubbed off on the Archangels.

'What did he say to you?' Michael asked.

'He said he was sorry.'

Gabriel made eye contact with Michael. They were all thinking the leader of the underworld would never be sorry.

'He also asked me what love felt like.' She looked at Gabriel.

'Berenike, he's trying to trick you. I don't want to speak of this again,' said Michael.

As the Archangels disappeared before them, Berenike was furious at her father's dismissal of her.

'Well, Father has spoken, and I will do as I'm told like a good girl. I swear, Gabriel, he still sees me as a child.'

Gabriel smirked. 'You're certainly not that, dear one.' As they sat together on the lounge, he took her hand and asked her nervously, 'So, what did you say to Jovan?'

'Does it matter?' Berenike couldn't shake her anger toward Michael.

'Come here, dear one.' Gabriel took Berenike's hand, pulled her body in closer to his, and held her as she calmed down.

'I can't believe he just dismissed me like that, Gabe.'

'Dear one, your mother's death changed him. Losing you was another blow for him, and now having you back with us...well, it's understandable how protective he is of you.'

'As protective as you are?' Gabriel couldn't help smiling.

Gabriel and Berenike both heard Michael's voice as he called for Gabriel to return to Heaven, and he kissed her hand as he disappeared. She smiled as they parted, and she could feel her heart pounding like it was about to jump out of her chest.

CHAPTER FOURTEEN

HOPE

Berenike returned to Heaven and began to wander the halls of the Heavenly Palace. As she explored, she could sense a familiar feeling coming from one of the rooms. She was a part of the heavens now, and her spiritual radar could sense the Archangels close by.

As she entered the room, she noticed Uriel standing there in a trance. He looked straight ahead; his eyes had clouded white, and the beams of white light that projected from his body had a magnificent glow. Berenike remembered the light beams she'd seen when she died as she passed from Earth into the realm of Heaven; they were the same. She slowly approached him and moved in close until she stood right under his chin. Uriel's statuesque figure towered over her.

Berenike found Uriel quite difficult to understand. He was extremely professional for a being of light, but he was also very handsome. His masculine energy and stature made her nervous. She stood there for what seemed like minutes, staring at him. Her curiosity began to get the better of her.

'How long are you going to stand there for, Berenike?'

As he snapped out of the trance and looked down at her, he took her by surprise. His booming voice frightened her, and she screamed and lost her footing. He stepped closer towards her as she scrambled to get away from him. His towering presence and gruff manner made her feel nervous around him; he wasn't like Gabriel or her father. There was something different about him. He was strong and stern, yet he radiated good. He was a complete contradiction. Uriel's presence was frightening to her, and she couldn't work out why. He had a strong sense of who the Archangels were and did his duty to God and the Heavens. Berenike felt transparent, as she knew he could see right through her.

'Are you all right?' He held out his hand to her and smiled. She said nothing as her hand stayed by her side, and Uriel's smile disappeared. 'You're frightened of me.' He was shocked at her reaction, and a little disappointed. He wasn't expecting to feel fear from her. 'I really don't mean to frighten you.' He didn't want her to be uncomfortable around him, so he changed the subject, trying to make conversation with her. 'I see you've been wandering the halls here.'

'How do you know what I've been doing?'

'Your father asked me to keep an eye on you.' Berenike raised an eyebrow, not sure how to receive the comment. 'Please don't let that bother you. He just wants to keep you safe. I spend a lot of time here. Why don't I show you around?' he said enthusiastically.

Uriel was enjoying spending time with her, and she remained silent and watched him as she let him guide her through the library and archives of Heaven.

'This is really quite magnificent. They look really old.'

'They are. Some of them are centuries old and even date back to the beginning of creation,' explained Uriel. 'Metatron is the caretaker of the archives and the chief scribe here in Heaven. He keeps record of all the comings and goings here. I really enjoy coming here. It's peaceful.'

Uriel had a sense of calm about him as he walked beside her. She could see him relax. He observed her carefully as they walked together.

'So, this is where you hide?' Berenike asked. Uriel smiled. 'So, what exactly is in these books?'

He could sense her fear was subsiding. 'Most of them are history books written about the old times of Earth. About Heaven and the beginning of civilisation. In fact, I'd highly recommend you start reading some of them, and right at the top you'll find all the Akashic records.'

Berenike looked up and could see there was no way she was going to reach any of the books that were before her. 'So, how do I get to them?'

'I'll show you,' Uriel said, smiling. He closed his eyes. 'Just think of the subject you're looking for and call it to you.'

Berenike watched Uriel as a book left the shelf above and fell into his hands. She then held out her hand and thought of what she wanted.

'Book,' she said.

Uriel couldn't help laughing at her. She was still human in so many ways.

'Berenike, you're an Archangel. You don't need to use words. Use your mind.'

Uriel wanted her to use her telepathic gifts to retrieve the book. She frowned and decided to try again. She thought of what she wanted to read. Berenike wanted to read about Jovan. She waited for a book to fall to her; nothing happened.

Uriel knew what she was after. 'You can't save him, Berenike. He's too far gone. That's why the books will not come to you; there is nothing written on him. God not only banished him from this Kingdom, he dissolved his name from all writings and scripture.'

'Maybe that's why he's so pissed at him,' she said under her breath. 'You know, it's rude to read a girl's mind, Uriel.'

'I didn't. I just took a guess,' he said with a grin. 'Berenike, Jovan and I were friends many years ago. We all loved him. If I thought I could save him, I would have done it a long time ago. Uriel and the Archangels were sad over Jovan's betrayal of God and the inhabitants of Heaven. He betrayed all of us, Berenike, not just God.'

'I'll find a way, Uriel. I promise you. I'll put this family back together.'

He wasn't sure what to say to her, but he could see she meant every word.

'Is it OK if I have a look around?'

'Of course. I'll show you the rest of the archives later if you like.' He sounded excited.

Berenike placed her hand on his arm 'Thank you, Uriel. I'd like that.'

'Please don't be afraid of me. I would like to be your friend, Berenike.'

His hand touched her cheek as he smiled. The stern Archangel she'd seen had virtually disappeared before her eyes. To him, she was captivating.

Gabriel was standing guard in the throne room when Uriel entered.

Berenike's conversations with Uriel had troubled him, and he watched him as he entered the room.

'What is it?' Gabriel was curious as to what could bother Uriel to this extent.

'What makes you think something's wrong?' Uriel snapped back.

'Well, I can feel it. There's enough worry coming off you to knock me over.'

Uriel took a deep breath. 'She's scared of me, Gabriel.'

'Uriel, that will change. Don't let it bother you. You're still getting to know each other.'

'She still thinks she can save him.'

'I know.' Gabriel was concerned. He stood in silence with Uriel, side by side as they looked out amongst the Heavens.

'Gabriel, don't you ever wonder?'

'Every single day, my friend. But the being we knew doesn't exist anymore. The Morning Star is gone. Jovan is different now.' Gabriel's mind drifted back to how Heaven used to be, with them all standing side by side. 'They were different times back then.'

'Then why is he connecting with Berenike? Why is he reaching out to her?' Uriel asked. 'It's more than just her light.'

'I don't know, but I do know she is the key to it all and we need to protect her.' Gabriel's response was never more serious.

'Agreed.' As Uriel proceeded to leave the throne room, he made one last statement that embedded doubt into Gabriel's mind. 'What if she's not wrong?'

Gabriel kept his focus looking out into the grounds of Heaven. 'What if her light can save him instead of destroy him?'

'Indeed.'

CHAPTER FIFTEEN

FAITH

Jovan's boldness during his visit to Berenike had shaken the Archangels. Gabriel remained in the throne room, deep in thought. He couldn't shake his concern for Berenike.

'You seem overly troubled, Gabriel,' said God. 'Tell me what's on your mind.' God had a watchful eye on the situation and was very aware of Jovan's encounters with Berenike. 'You know I see all.'

Gabriel couldn't contain his emotions any further. 'Lord, I'm worried for her, and I'm concerned for the Heavens. I can sense the situation worsening,' Gabriel gushed.

God could see his concern. 'Since when, my beautiful Archangel, have you not had the faith to believe the outcome will be better than you could have imagined? Why have you lost faith? I think some of Berenike's humanity is rubbing off on you.' God was becoming concerned. 'This worry is not good for my Archangel.

Gabriel, what is the one thing you know from being in my Kingdom?' He asked him.

Gabriel bowed his head. He felt like a scalded child who had let his father down. 'Lord, you always say there's a reason for everything that happens.'

'Indeed, there is. Gabriel, don't lose faith, especially in her.' God was concerned. He could see the bond forming between them. 'Berenike will become the being written of in the archives, and you will have a role in that. Just as you need to remember who you are, she will need to realise who she is destined to be and not be afraid of it.' He

God was beginning to see how Berenike's arrival in Heaven had turned Gabriel's world completely upside down. He affectionately placed his hand on Gabriel's shoulder.

'Gabriel, you are not her father. Let Michael do all the worrying. Just be what she needs. Be her friend, and the rest will fall into place. You'll see.' Gabriel realised God already knew how he felt about Berenike. 'My beautiful Archangel, teach her. She is new to our world. Teach her to be strong with you by her side,' said God.

Gabriel was surprised at his request.

God sat back on his throne and smiled at Gabriel, who was wondering if God could see through him. If his love for Berenike would be forbidden because of his duty to Heaven, as was Michael's relationship with Sarra. The Archangels could all see how Gabriel felt for her, and her father knew his daughter was in love.

Michael, Raphael, and Uriel all entered the throne room.

'Michael, how is Berenike fitting in?' God asked. He was curious to see how her father was adjusting to her arrival.

'Lord, she's fitting in quite well. We've all been spending time with her. It's important she get to spend time with all of us so she feels safe, especially when I'm not around.' Michael was proud of his daughter. He was acting like a parent, and he didn't even realise it.

God grinned.

'Spoken like a true parent.'

They all laughed. Berenike's arrival had brought joy to them all throughout the Heavenly Kingdom.

'She's learning quickly, and she's mastering her gifts at a rapid rate.'

'Michael, she always was an intelligent being. She is the daughter of an Archangel and a High Priestess, not to mention being half-human. There are those who will view her as a prize, Michael, a very valuable prize, and you need to protect her. In the wrong hands, she can be used as a weapon, you know that.' God was concerned they'd be lax and let their guard down while protecting her.

'No,' said Gabriel. 'She has too much light in her to ever turn to darkness.'

'Where is she now?' God asked them.

Uriel's eyes shaded white and his body beamed with the light of God as he searched for her. Finally, he smiled. 'I believe she's walking through the city centre, she's exploring. I've never seen a soul with that much curiosity in them before.'

As Uriel used his abilities and gift of sight to see where she was, Raphael stood forward. 'Lord, I spoke to her earlier and suggested she get to know some of the folks in the city.' Michael was surprised at his comments. 'She misses her friends, Michael.' Raphael could feel her sadness at the loss of her old life.

'I think that's a very good idea, Raphael,' said God. 'We all need to remember that her human traits are more dominant than her

Angelic side now. That will change though. She does not know how to be an Archangel, so we need to make the adjustment as easy as possible for her, and quickly. It's up to all of you to teach her.'

They all bowed before God at his command.

'She's curious about the palace, and about you, Lord,' said Gabriel. 'I find her staring up at it from a distance quite often.'

'How much of the Palace has she seen?'

'She's only been as far as the archives, Lord. We haven't shown her the great staircase yet,' explained Uriel.

'When can I bring her before you, Lord?' Michael asked. He was curious as well.

'Not yet. Soon, but not yet.'

Michael was a little disappointed. He was proud of Berenike and wanted to present his daughter to his maker.

Metatron entered the throne room and took his place next to God, who could sense he was troubled.

'Why are all my Archangels so troubled this day?' He could see and feel the distress rising within them.

'Lord, we need to discuss Jovan,' said Metatron.

With the visitations to Berenike, they all felt it was time to plan a strategy to protect the Heavens.

'Yes, Metatron. He will try again, and you will have to fight back. I cannot predict what will happen next, but I do know he has a legion prepared. I have been watching him. We must be ready for him, and for all possibilities.'

God knew they all had to band together. It was more important now than ever before. Berenike's arrival in Heaven would now give them a fighting chance against him.

'Lord, I would like to put all guardians on alert at each level of the palace.'

Michael was concerned. His tactical mind was working

overtime with battle strategies. He knew they would need to perfect a battle plan to prepare for any attack Jovan would throw at them.

'Good idea, Michael.' God nodded in agreement with his request.

As Michael spoke to the Archangels, they all listened. 'You all need to remember, as much as we have to protect the humans, we also have a duty to protect the souls here in Heaven. If he infiltrates the grounds and gets into the palace, there is a chance we will fall. There is no room for failure, remember that. Heaven cannot fall into darkness.' They could all see the worry on Michael's face. 'Our lord must be protected at all times.'

'It won't, my friend. I promise you,' said Metatron. I

Metatron shared Michael's concerns, but he knew the power they had in their bond as Archangels. When needed, they would stand side by side in defence of Eternity.

CHAPTER SIXTEEN

Berenike walked through the centre of the Heavenly city. She observed the congregations of beings as she passed by several of the Angels she'd met while basking in God's light. She said hello, waved to some of the familiar faces as she passed through the city, and within minutes she realised she'd wandered into a graveyard. It was bleak and cold and nowhere familiar compared to what she'd previously seen.

It seemed strange to her a place full of so much happiness and light could have a glimmer of darkness dwelling within it. This wasn't a usual area of Heaven that was visited, and she began to wonder if she should wander any further.

She walked and walked, looking at each headstone and the symbols that replaced what would normally occupy the names of the deceased as they did on Earth. She couldn't read any of it at this point.

'Go and get my daughter. Get her out of there now,' Michael said to Metatron. He was furious.

'Don't be angry at her, Michael,' said God. 'She's just exploring. Inquisitive, isn't she?' God smiled as he placed his hand on Michael's shoulder.

God found Berenike behaviour fascinating. They both continued to watch her as she read over every tombstone and walked further and further until she reached a wall of light; it was Metatron, who'd materialized in front of her.

'That's as far as you can go, Berenike,' said Metatron. 'You shouldn't be here.'

'What exactly is here?'

'This is the ancient burial ground for Ascended Masters. No one enters here. It is sacred. This is a space where God has laid his prophet's Earthly bodies to rest. This ground is only accessible to the Archangels or God himself.'

'Well, I'm part Archangel, so that means it's OK, huh?'

Metatron grinned as she continued to inspect the headstones. He couldn't argue with her. The grounds Berenike had entered were separate from the more populated areas of Heaven. They were sacred grounds and isolated from most of the population.

'No wonder nobody comes here; it's so bleak and gloomy.' The darkness that surrounded the gravesite gave her body a chill as she tingled from head to toe.

'Why does no one visit here to pay his or her respects? On Earth, that's something we do when someone has passed.'

'It's Gods command, Berenike, and we obey,' Metatron said. His tone of voice had lowered towards her. He understood what she was saying perfectly. It made sense to him.

'Just because they've moved on doesn't mean we forget about them, Metatron,' she said sternly.

Berenike manifested a bunch of the brightest sunflowers for every tombstone she could see. The yellow of the flowers had radiated such a glow, everyone in Heaven could see it in the distance from where they were. The dirt on the ground was unattended and was nothing more than dust. The grass had wilted to the roots. With a raise of her hand, she transformed the dirt to a healthy layer of lush green grass. Metatron was surprised but welcomed her heartfelt gesture. He smiled at her as he could see her heart radiating love for the beings who had ascended.

'Now that's better.'

Michael and God looked on. God smiled and chuckled under his breath.

'She truly is a treasure. I think she'll have much to teach us, Michael. I'm looking forward to meeting her.'

Michael couldn't help smiling.

As they left the sacred burial grounds, Berenike and Metatron chatted about what the old times were like in Heaven. She was very curious about all the Archangels.

'Metatron, what do the symbols say on the headstones?'

'Child, it's what we call light language. All beings in the universe can read it, and so will you very soon.'

'And what about you, Metatron?'

'What do you mean, child?'

'What's it like to be a powerful Archangel?' she asked enthusiastically.

'What's it like to be a child of God's light?'

He laughed. 'Honestly, it's hard work, but it's amazing and frightening, all at the same time. I remember what it used to be like, and I remember how frightening it was when I became an Archangel.'

'I've read you used to be human, is it true?'

'Yes, Berenike, I was once, and for my work serving our lord, I was rewarded and ascended to be an Archangel. I am very old, you know.'

'But you're very wise as well, I think.' She smiled at him.

'Where did you read that?' he asked.

'The Internet.'

Metatron couldn't help laughing at her comment. 'Humans,' he said, shaking his head as he laughed with her.

'Metatron, do Archangels die?'

Metatron had realised something was bothering her. There was a reason for all the questions. The closer she was getting to the Archangels, she was worried about losing them. She was worried about her Father, and of course Gabriel. Being in the graveyard had planted the seeds of worry in her mind. They'd all become such a part of her life now.

To Metatron, it seemed like a logical question to ask. Berenike still had many human traits about her, which made her easy to read. She'd been on her own for so long, to lose the only family she had would be unbearable to her now that her father was back in her life.

'We haven't yet, child.' He smiled. 'Don't worry yourself over that sort of thing. You need to remember, you do not live in a human world anymore. Life is different here.' They could both see Gabriel approaching in the distance. Metatron took this as his cue to leave. 'Go easy on him, won't you?' he said with a smile, then hugged her as he said goodbye. 'Oh, and thank you for the flowers,' he said, bowing as he left. Her gesture had broken the ice between the two of them.

'Which one were you?'

There was no answer. He would only smile.

'Hello, Gabriel,' she said. She was so happy to see him.

'Berenike, come, I need to speak with you.' Gabriel had a serious tone to his request.

'Have I done something wrong?'

'No, dear one. I need to know why you think you can save Jovan.'

'I saw something in him,' she said. She thought about him for a moment as Gabriel listened. 'It wasn't so much what he said to me; it was more the look in his eyes. The sadness that was there, especially when he apologised to me for my mother's death. Why do you want to know this now? You know my father has forbid me to talk about it.' She realised there was doubt in Gabriel's mind as she looked him in the eye. 'You think he can be saved, don't you?'

Gabriel couldn't bring himself to tell her both he and Uriel were having doubts about whether Jovan could return to the light.

'I'm worried about his visitations to you. You must promise me you will call for me the next time he comes to you. I can't lose you.'

'I promise.' She couldn't look at him, as his romantic gesture made her blush.

'Why is everyone so angry at me over this? Is it so unbelievable it just might be a possibility that we can save him?'

'Berenike, I love that fight in you, but you need to understand which battles you can and can't win. There won't always be a victory, dear one.' She nodded in agreement. 'Come, we need to do more training.' Berenike rolled her eyes. 'Come on.' He took her hand and led her to the training fields.

'I can think of other things I'd rather be using my energy on,' she said under her breath as Gabriel led her to the training grounds.

He grinned, hearing every word she said.

CHAPTER SEVENTEEN

THE PLAN

Hell became a hub of activity. Jovan's followers were rejoicing in the knowledge that soon they would be in control of the Heavens. Under Jovan's command, they would have the existence they used to know before their banishment. Jovan inspected swords and battle equipment as he moved between several chambers of Hell. They'd now accumulated a large supply of weapons.

'Minion, how is everything coming along? How long before we have enough swords?' Jovan was anxious for battle.

'We're almost done, Sire. Sire, what of the light child?'

'Not long now, and she will come to me, and then I can use her light and take the Heavens.'

'You will be where you belong, Sire. We all will. Sire, what will you do with her once you have Heaven?'

'Well, my friend, you keep asking me about a Queen, so I thought I might grant you that wish. I will make her the Queen of

Heaven. She has her father's strength. She's exactly what a Queen of our Kingdom should be - and Minion, I will make you the leader of my army.'

'Sire, I'm very honoured.' Minion bowed down before Jovan.

'Of course you are, my friend. You have been very loyal to me over the years. You deserve a reward.'

Jovan walked the halls of Hell, passing through the corridors of the cells that held beings from several millennia. All the prisoners contained in the dungeons in hell were dark souls that had committed crimes, wrongdoers, and those who corrupted the souls of the innocent. Within the walls was a collection of beings that hadn't ascended to heaven. They found the perfect home in Hell.

As Jovan walked from level to level, he passed each locked cell and opened every one of them, releasing the beings that dwelled there.

'You've all been caged too long. I am building an army to take the Heavens and regain control of our home. You will have everything you desire. Be a part of my Kingdom. Are you with me!?' he yelled.

Every evil being throughout the cell block was cheering in support of their future King. 'Jovan! Jovan!' the voices cried out throughout the epicentre of Hell. His numbers were many, and his followers were rejoicing in the thought of returning to the light from which they came.

'It is only a matter of time now before I come home, Michael,' he yelled, 'and I will have what belongs to me, including your daughter. Minion!' he yelled. 'Tonight we celebrate.'

As the evening progressed, the inhabitants of Hell began to celebrate. Minion watched his master and King become more distracted as his followers celebrated the impending takeover of the Heavens. Alcohol flowed, and the beasts that dwelled within the confines of the walls beneath the Earth celebrated. The beings that dwelled there were the lowest of life forms that had ever walked the face of the Earth.

As Jovan took a walk around the grounds of Hell, his mind drifted back to his memories of his life in Heaven. As memories flooded back, sadness swept over him. Jovan remembered the light. He closed his eyes as he remembered the light of God shining on his face while he stretched out his beautiful wings as he shone brightly. The faces of the children and animals that inhabited the only place in existence he'd ever had inner peace, love, and acceptance.

The Archangels were his family. Many who knew him, loved him. The one he missed the most, though, was God himself. God was his Father, his creator. Jovan was feeling regret for his actions. He missed his life in Heaven, but the more he thought about it, the angrier he became. Jovan thought he should be in charge, and he wanted to claim his inheritance. He wanted to be the leader, and he wanted to make God proud. Unfortunately, his jealousy was more powerful than his urge to want to please God.

Jovan slammed his fist against the wall as he screamed. His anger was heard throughout the depths of hell.

'Minion, I want everyone ready. Tonight we celebrate, and then we take Earth.'

Minion smiled as his King was finally ready to take his command as King of the heavens.

'And then the Kingdom of Jovan will begin,' Jovan seethed.

CHAPTER EIGHTEEN

EARTHLY PLANE

Amy was slowly getting on top of Berenike's business affairs. If anything, it had taught her to make sure her own affairs were in order just in case anything was to happen, just like they did to Berenike.

As Amy wandered around the shop, she saw the remnants of a life now passed; the life Berenike had shared with her and EJ.

Amy found it hard to mourn her friend, as she'd already come to her as a spirit. As far as she was concerned, Berenike wasn't dead. EJ knew it would be hard for Amy to work her way through the paperwork. She wasn't a business owner, but as EJ had a business background, it would make it easier to understand with his help. As EJ looked through record after record, he couldn't find a single fault.

'You know her books are immaculate. I can't find anything wrong, no errors at all.' EJ was a little surprised.

'Berenike was always really thorough. I guess that's why this place was so profitable. She was very much the professional. I wonder what she's doing up there?' Amy smiled to herself.

'You know she's always going to be with you.' EJ picked up a photo of Amy and Berenike together on one of their nights out and passed the photo frame to her. 'I miss her too,' he said as he passed the frame to her, 'but I feel like she's still here. I guess that's because we saw her.'

EJ couldn't mourn her either. It was an odd feeling, but they knew they were luckier than many others who 'd gone through the grief of losing a loved one. Amy stopped what she was doing and sat down with EJ.

'EJ, I feel so guilty,' she said.

'Why?'

'For the last two thousand or so years, we've been taught about God and religion, and many of us still don't believe in the possibility that there actually is a being that created everything, let alone the idea of Heaven or what happens after we die. Why is it we never give that a thought? I feel bad that it took me to see her to believe in it.' EJ had never seen Amy so sullen. 'I think I finally understand.'

'I guess God gave us free will to spice things up a bit. I still don't know what I believe or what it'll take for me to believe, but I do know Berenike came to us, with a warning.'

'I know; I've been thinking about that. What do you think is going on up there?' Amy's concern showed as she frowned. 'I'm more worried about what's going on down there.'

EJ was deeply worried about Berenike's warning. Human beings already had an untouched level of intuition ingrained into who they were. They just had to remember where they came from. They both knew Jovan was coming, and soon.

'So, what do you want to do with this place, Amy?' Neither of them had time to run the business themselves.

'Well, we should re-open it, and soon. I'll hire a manager.' No sooner had they spoke, the room began to shake. As they both held on to each other, they knew it was time.

'Everyone to the surface!' Jovan commanded. 'Minion, I want you to stay and guard my Kingdom.' Minion agreed. 'Rise up and claim what is yours, my friends. Leave no human untouched.'

Jovan was smiling from ear to ear, seething, as he gave his command. He sat on his throne, observing the joy radiating off the prisoners who occupied hell.

As the sun began to hide, Amy and EJ looked out the window of Berenike's store. They watched as Jovan forced an eclipse and placed the Earth into total darkness. They then locked the store and knew Berenike wouldn't be too far away.

'She'll come looking for us, so we need to get back to the house,' said EJ.

They drove as fast as they could. As they reached Berenike's house, they ran inside to find Muffin hiding in a corner, shaking. Amy held her in her arms while EJ used whatever he could find to barricade the front and back door.

As EJ looked outside, he could see the beings who'd once inhabited Hell now walking the Earth. His face said it all. There were people running, frantically screaming and trying to get away from the beasts and demons running down the street. The screams were deafening.

'Where are they? Why aren't they here protecting us?'

Amy screamed as the glass from the windows shattered. Where were the Archangels? And where was Berenike?

CHAPTER NINETEEN

DARKNESS FALLS

As Gabriel escorted Berenike into the training fields of Heaven, he could sense she was becoming annoyed with the constant practice and lessons.

'OK, so we know you can fly, create and manifest, and have the light within you,' he said. 'So now let's see you direct the light.'

Gabriel paced the field. The closer he was to her physically, the more he fought how he felt for her. By the smiles on their faces, it was obvious they loved spending time together. Berenike directed the light and successfully projected it at the targets Gabriel had set up. She was bored. She craved to do something adventurous.

'That's my girl. Well done.'

'Your girl, huh?' Berenike glanced over at Gabriel to find him staring back at her. Her comment certainly got his attention. 'So how much more training does your girl need, exactly?' she asked with a hint of sarcasm. Berenike was annoyed at his constant observance of her combat skills.

Gabriel said softly, 'We need to keep practicing.'

'Gabe, why don't you want to spend any time with me?

He stopped what he was doing to talk to her. She didn't want to train; she just wanted to spend time with him, like they did when they walked through the gardens together. They were becoming inseparable, but today he was different. She could see that yearning in his eyes to be with her. He gave her the same look when she arrived in Heaven. She stood there, waiting for his answer.

'For goodness sake, Gabriel, that's it; I'm not doing this anymore.' Berenike stood defiant before him with her arms folded, then turned her back to walk away.

'Berenike, you need to be ready for him. We aren't doing this for fun. You're doing this so you stand a fighting chance against him!' he yelled.

Berenike had never seen Gabriel angry before, yet there was a sense of desperation in his statement as well. 'I don't want anything to happen to you, dear one. None of us does.'

Berenike placed her hand on his heart, nodding in agreement with him.

'I'm sorry. I didn't mean to upset you.' She stood close to him and could feel his breath getting closer to her face.

'Why don't we take a break for a few minutes?' Gabriel said. 'Come with me. I want to show you something. I think it will help you understand better.'

As he took her into his arms, she swallowed hard. The moment he touched her, her heart raced with excitement.

'Hold on.'

With Berenike in his arms, Gabriel spread his magnificent wings and took flight into the light of Heaven. The smile on her face was beaming. He took her higher and higher into the sky, an impressive sight as he flew into the Heavens with his wings stretched out.

'Where are you taking me?' she asked.

Gabriel smiled, then flew them higher and higher until they were out of sight. He stopped mid-flight, then closed his eyes as he rested his cheek against hers.

'Look around. I want you to see what I see.'

Berenike did as he asked. As she looked down beneath her, she could see the inhabitants of her new home. As she looked out across the Heavens, she could feel the love within each heart, the children laughing as they frolicked with their pets in the fields, and an abundance of angelic beings that radiated the light from God.

'Berenike, this is what I'm fighting for, what we all must fight for. You're a part of this world now, a part of my world.' She hugged him a little tighter. 'Heaven must exist. Without it, there is nothing but darkness. The balance must remain!'

Gabriel worried enough for them both, with what was to come. All he could think of was how to keep her safe from harm. They'd touched each other's hearts in so many ways.

'When you make a statement, Gabe, you go all out, don't you? I understand.'

Berenike remained in his embrace as they took the journey back to the training grounds. As they touched the ground, neither of them was in a hurry to let go of the other. She couldn't bring herself to break away from him as she held him tighter.

'Please don't let go.'

'Never.' He drew in a breath as he smiled to himself, then abruptly stepped away from her. Berenike could see fear on his face.

'What is it? What's wrong?' she asked. She could see the light diminishing around her. 'Why is it getting dark?'

'It's not here; it's Earth. What has he done now?' Gabriel said as he held Berenike's hand as tightly as he could. 'Stay close to me.' She nodded.

They headed back to the combat room in the Heavenly Palace, where the other Archangels were preparing to head to Earth. Berenike arrived to find her father and the Archangels in full battle uniform. As she stood there watching, Gabriel helped her prepare her armour for battle. She reached out to her Father.

'It's starting, isn't it?'

Berenike was scared, and Michael could sense her fear. He couldn't answer her. 'Gabriel, do not let her out of your sight,' he stressed.

'All right, listen up, everyone. We do not know what we are going to find down there, but the priority is to defend humanity. He'll be coming for Berenike, so all of you need to look out for her.' Everyone agreed. 'He won't be expecting her to have any fighting skills, so at least she can defend herself to some extent against him.'

'I'll protect her,' Gaige said as he moved closer to stand beside Berenike.

'It's all right, Gaige. I've got that covered,' said Gabriel, who smiled at Berenike as she stood closer to his side.

Gaige could see something was going on between them. It was clear Gaige wasn't a priority in her life now, nor was he a second thought. As the jealousy was emerging within him, his coldness towards them both began to show.

'Are we ready?' asked Michael as he placed his arms around his daughter and held his child. 'Stay strong, and remember who you are,' he said. 'Gabriel, take her.'

As the ground shook and glass shattered, the sky was now dark all over the world. Darkness fell, drawing every living being outside and onto the streets. Jovan had managed to call all evil to the surface of Earth, and as the veil between the two worlds disappeared, everything became visible. The fear was overwhelming to its inhabitants. To humanity, they'd found Armageddon. As darkness fell, the angels were also visible and the Kingdom of Heaven could be seen high up in the sky.

'Remember, if we get separated, you call for me, all right?'

'Be safe, Gabriel.' Berenike kissed his cheek.

'What is it? Where are you going?'

'I need to find Amy and EJ. Will you come with me?'

Gabriel could see how worried she was and knew she was determined to find her friends.

'Of course.'

CHAPTER TWENTY

HUMANITY

Berenike needed to see her friends. At this point, their safety was the only thing she could focus on.

'Gabriel, how do I find them?'

'Remember, just close your eyes and think about what you want. It's like manifesting, but instead of an object, you have a destination. You want to go to them? Take us there.,' he said as he held on to her while she transported them to her friends.

Berenike opened her eyes. She'd taken them both to her house, where EJ and Amy had come to hide with the hope they might run into her. As Gabriel and Berenike materialised before them, Amy leaped up from the floor where she was hiding.

'Thank God you're OK,' Amy said, hugging Berenike as tightly as she could. 'We were so worried about you.'

Berenike smiled. 'I'm fine.'

Amy and EJ were startled by the sight of Gabriel, who appeared before them with his wings stretched out behind him.

'Gabe, why don't you put them away for a little while? They haven't actually seen an Archangel before; it's a little scary for them.'

'Didn't your father appear to them?' Gabe asked.

'Yes, but he appeared as a man, not an Angel,' Berenike raised her eyebrow as she explained to him.

'Oh, I see.' Gabriel immediately retracted his wings and tucked them into his back. His aura could still be seen where his wings were, but now he looked like one of them; human.

Berenike smiled as he winked at her. 'Guys, this is my friend Gabriel. He's an Archangel, just like my father. Gabe, these are my friends, Amy and EJ.'

Gabriel smiled and bowed his head to them. As Amy glanced at Gabriel, she saw the look on her friend's face and smirked.

'Friend, huh? Right,' she said as she began to laugh, then hugged her friend. 'Do you realise you're glowing? You never were very good at hiding your feelings. I don't need to be an angel to see your heart.' Amy smiled as she glanced at Gabriel. 'He's very handsome,' Amy whispered as they both giggled.

'EJ, are you OK?' Gabe asked. EJ just stood in shock at the sight of the Archangel. 'Why don't you tell me when this all started.' Gabriel had to say something to snap him out of shock from seeing his wings.

'Well, it's been odd over the last 24 hours. There's an excessive amount of fighting and a lot of unrest in the world. More than usual; not the amount we normally have, anyway. News reports have been nonstop with one story after another. But the earthquakes make sense after what we've all just seen.'

'What do you mean?' Gabriel asked.

'The demons came out of the ground when the sky went black,

and they started killing everyone. Most of us just ran for cover. We came here because we knew Berenike would come and find us.'

'It sounds like they waited for his command. The closer evil is to good, the more it upsets the balance. With that much evil on the Earth, it's no wonder there was such upheaval,' said Gabriel. 'EJ, Amy', he paused, 'you're both going to have to fight.'

'We know. Berenike warned us.'

As the Archangels appeared before Amy and EJ, Berenike signaled them to put their wings away, as she did with Gabriel. As Amy saw Gaige standing side by side with them, she could feel herself building with rage.

'You're one of them! This entire time, you were one of them while you were breaking her heart!' Amy was furious at him.

'It's in the past, Amy. Let's leave it there, OK? We have more important things to worry about right now,' Berenike said to her friend.

Amy was worried. No sooner had she yelled at Gaige, she saw the look on Gabriel's face. 'You need to keep him away from her. There's something not quite right about him.'

'Agreed,' said Gabriel.

Amy calmed herself down and stood side by side with her friend.

'Guy , these are my friends, Amy and EJ,' Berenike said to the Archangels. As she turned to her friends, she said with pride, 'And these are the Archangels of the lord. This is Metatron, Raphael, and Uriel.' They all bowed to her friends. 'You've already met my father, Michael.'

'Hello again.'

EJ was stunned. 'It's all true. Everything we were taught as children...it's all true.'

'It's so much more than just a story, EJ. Heaven is incredible. It's pure love,' Berenike said as she embraced her friend.

'All right, the two of you can talk about Heaven later. Right now, we need to get serious,' said Michael. 'The Earth is in danger, and now that Jovan has broken through the veil here, he will stop at nothing to infiltrate Heaven and destroy God.'

'How is that possible?' said Amy. 'You can't destroy God.'

'Amy, he's planning on using the light from within Berenike. If he can't obtain that, he will more than likely use force.' Amy froze. Michael continued. 'It's always been something that's been feared, but I think we now know nothing is impossible,' Michael said as he smiled at his daughter.

'We need everyone to fight,' said Metatron as he gathered weapons. 'There's no way he's going to stop now.'

'So, if we can see demons, then everybody can see Angels as well?' Amy asked.

'Yes, Amy,' said Michael.

'Well, that explains what the other beings are out there on the streets.'

'What do you mean?' Raphael asked.

'You obviously haven't looked outside yet.'

Raphael looked beyond the window to see a massacre of bodies on the sidewalk outside Berenike's home. An infantry of angels had all travelled to Earth to help but had perished amongst the fighting. Raphael bowed his head in honour of those souls already perished at the hands of evil.

'So many,' he whispered to himself.

'How long do you think we have before he comes for me, Father?' Berenike asked. Everyone was concerned for her. She knew the time would come for her to confront Jovan. 'I'm worried about my friends.'

Michael stopped what he was doing to address his daughter. 'Your focus needs to remain on Jovan. You know how to use your light, so you need to stay focused on him. Let us protect your friends.'

Berenike nodded in agreement, and the room went silent as he embraced her Father. Michael cupped his daughter's face in his hands as he fought back tears.

'Don't you say goodbye to me. I won't allow it.'

Michael's emotional declaration had everyone realising the seriousness of the situation. They all knew how much he loved his daughter.

Gaige stood in the background, scowling at Gabriel. He was green with envy, and his hatred for Gabriel was showing.

The Archangels each took a sword as the Earth began to shake, then Gabriel took hold of Berenike's hand and they ran outside onto the street.

CHAPTER TWENTY-ONE

RAGE AND EVIL

As Berenike and Gabriel took their positions on the street, the Archangels followed.

'Spread out and help who you can,' yelled Michael.

As the Archangels set out to save humanity, Gaige was keeping a very close eye on Berenike and Gabriel. His jealousy was slowly aligning with his rage.

'Gaige, focus on the streets. Gabriel is looking after her now,' said Michael.

Gaige was furious. After all the years he'd been her protector, he felt it was his right to be by Berenike's side. He wanted to claim her affections now that everything had changed. He ran into the crowd battling the demons that had risen to the surface of the Earth, his blade clashing as he released his anger towards the beasts that occupied the streets.

'I want you to stay close to us,' Berenike said to EJ and Amy. 'If we get separated, I want you to hide at the house and stay there until we find you, OK? Just stick together.' They both nodded to her.

The Earth continued to erupt, and the ground in front of them began to separate. As Gabriel and Berenike stood there watching, the fear began to cripple her and she froze.

'Berenike!' Gabriel yelled as loud as he could, trying to snap her attention back to what was about to arrive.

Berenike began to tremble. Jovan had risen out of the Earth and stood at the end of the street. As he marched the straight length of the street like a missile, his focus remained on her. Jovan raised his hand to deliver the command, shooting a beam of dark light at Gabriel and sending him flying across the street away from Berenike. In response, she raised her hand to guide the light to him, and the shot of light thrust him across the street away from her and her friends.

'Run, go and help the children. Get them inside! Go! Now!' she yelled at them.

Jovan got up; Berenike's attack seemed to encourage him even more. He came towards her again, this time with his sword in hand, and began to fight. Berenike remembered her training and fought him with every ounce of strength she had. The blades clashed as the shine from her sword blinded him. Without a moment's thought, Berenike ran so she could get him off the streets. She knew he would follow her, and he did, moving swiftly after her. With the streets still in darkness, it made it easier to hide.

As Berenike ran through the darkness of the streets, she decided to work out a strategy of how to get Jovan alone to tap into his angelic side. Berenike was more determined than ever to turn him back to God's light.

'Berenike, you're wasting time playing games with me. Let's talk.' Jovan walked down the alleyway. 'There's no point in hiding from me. I can feel you.' He'd found her but remained silent in the darkness. She knew what she had to do. She could feel he was close.

'I can help you return to the light. Please let me help you, Jovan.'

He stepped into the night light so she could see him before her. He stood tall next to her.

'I can save you from the darkness. I know in my heart you want to feel that light on your face again. Just take my hand, and we can walk out of here together. You can say goodbye to the darkness.' She could see the tears well in his eyes.

Jovan ran both hands over her arms and held her wrists within his hand. He began to squeeze as she tried to struggle out of his grip.

'You little fool, do you think God will forgive me for what I've done?!'

'Your family wants you to come home, and so do I,' she said.

Just as she thought her words were making a difference to him, he pulled his sword from behind his back and stabbed her in the stomach. Berenike wrestled with him, and as she twisted to get away from him, he broke her arm. She screamed as she struggled to get away from his grip, then raised her hand and shot a beam of light at him that sent him to the other end of the alleyway as she ran out of sight.

'I'll find you, Berenike!' Jovan screamed.

Gabriel searched everywhere for Berenike. He was worried he couldn't connect with her. He found Amy and EJ hiding with a group of children in an abandoned house.

'Have you seen her?'

'No, she told us to take cover somewhere if we got separated. When Jovan came out of the ground, she told us to run,' said Amy.

'I can't find her.' The distress on Gabriel's face worried Amy, who could see EJ was comforting several children from the sight of Gabriel.

'Gabriel, how do you normally find her?'

'She's in my heart. I normally just know where she is, but I can't sense her.'

'You need to stay calm and focus. Your emotions must be clouding your connection to her. Find the others. Find Michael.'

He nodded in agreement. 'Stay here,' he said as he left to find Berenike.

Gabriel appeared before Michael. 'I can't find her,' he said to her father.

'What do you mean?' Michael was worried.

'Jovan came for her. She managed to get him off the streets, but they disappeared before I could get back to them,' he said.

'I swear, if he's hurt her, I'll kill him myself!' Gabriel said.

His declaration shocked Michael. 'Gabriel, I know you care for my daughter, but this isn't helping her. She needs you with a clear head. We need to find her. Gaige, come with me,' said Michael as they left to try to locate Berenike.

'Well done, Gabriel,' said Gaige, who would now take the opportunity to play on Michael's emotions.

Gabriel's guilt was overwhelming, as he tried to communicate with her. 'Berenike, call for me...where are you?' he asked desperately.

CHAPTER TWENTY-TWO

A FATHER'S LOVE

Berenike lay on the ground in an alleyway, hidden behind a garbage bin. Her breathing became heavy as she struggled to keep awake. Her wounds were taking their toll on her body. She could feel the energy drain her from within from the shock of her wounds. Berenike knew if Jovan were to find her now, the results would be fatal in her weakened state. Berenike now had experienced her first attack from Jovan. He was a skilful fighter, but none of her training with Gabriel had prepared her for their encounter. She could feel her heart beating heavily as she rested her eyes, and as she heard Michael and Gaige talking, her exhaustion prevented her from yelling out.

'So, what's his story, Michael? Why does he want Berenike so badly? You've never really told me the full story,' Gaige said.

'As you know, Berenike is my daughter.'

'I do now, yes. Thanks for keeping that from me all these years, by the way.'

'Well, he knows Berenike is of the light and he can use the light within her as a weapon, like a gun, against God. Once he's done that, he can inflict darkness upon the Earth forever and control both Heaven and Hell and all its inhabitants. Gaige, he would also have control of the different dimensions of the universe. This cannot come to pass. Because Berenike is born of an Archangel and a human, it makes her very special. We don't yet know what she'll be capable of. He'll use her to his advantage if he ever convinces her to join him.'

'So that's why you gave her to me to look after.'

'Yes, well, it wasn't exactly the best of plans. He knew where she was the whole time. When God sent her away, I knew she would need protection,' Michael said as he continued to walk down the alleyway, looking for his daughter.

'I apologise for what I said to you earlier,' Gaige said.

'I'm not sorry I hit you. You had it coming for a long time,' said Michael.

'Still, it must have been hard for you to live without her?' As they both walked together down the alleyway, scanning for Berenike, Gaige asked, 'You kept it all pretty secret. I mean, I never knew of anything being said up there about you having a child with a mortal.'

'No, only the Archangels knew,' said Michael, disappointed. 'Sarra, Berenike's mother was known to us. She was loved and respected by many and was a great teacher and healer. She was different. She was not like most mortal beings. She was never afraid of us and would draw on our knowledge, and in turn would teach her followers.'

'Like a High Priestess?'

'Yes, a very powerful High Priestess, actually. Her family was well-respected and sought out through many lands for their knowledge of healing.'

It was all starting to make more sense to Gaige as Michael revealed what his heart wanted to say.

'I started to spend a great deal of time here on Earth. I loved being with her. It made me happy just to be in her presence. Unfortunately, Jovan became jealous. When Sarra didn't return his affections...well, things started to decline rapidly.'

'I found out Sarra was pregnant with our child. We named her Berenike. Ironically, it means "the bringer of victory". After she was born, Sarra begged me to take her and keep her safe. She was terrified Jovan would come after all three of us, especially our daughter. I returned to Heaven, but I could sense something was wrong.'

Michael's thoughts drifted back to where his nightmare began. He'd confided in Gabriel not only about his child, but also about the growing darkness within Jovan.

'Michael, how is this possible? Archangels do not have children. Especially with humans.'

'I don't know, but I do know this child within her is good. God always tells me there is a reason for everything he does, so this too has a purpose.'

'What has he foreseen, my friend?' Gabriel was curious.

'I don't know, Gabriel.'

Michael and Gabriel had been summoned, along with the other Archangels, to appear before God.

'I take it this is about my family?' said Michael.

'No, friend,' said Gabriel, 'we have other things to be worried about. The darkness surrounding Jovan is now of great concern to God. We think he will try and take the Heavens.'

'Are you sure? Why now, after all this time?' Michael could

sense the worry in his friend. 'God believes it has to do with Berenike.'

'Come, Michael.'

While the Archangels all congregated in Heaven in the holy court, Jovan decided to visit Sarra one last time.

'I don't have much time. Sarra, once again, I ask you to join me in my Kingdom. Take your place with me.' He held out his hand to her.

'Never!' she spat at him.

Jovan would make her suffer for refusing him.

Michael and Gabriel appeared in the Holy Court and joined the rest of the Archangels. They realised they'd walked into an intense argument over Berenike.

'She is an abomination, and I will not protect this thing,' said Metatron.

'You are a messenger of God; you will do as He has commanded,' Uriel said.

'Who are you to order me, Uriel?' Metatron was furious.

'Every child must be protected, Metatron. This child is no different,' said Uriel.

As Michael stood before his fellow Archangels, he couldn't believe what he was hearing.

'She is my child, yet you speak of her with such hatred,' Michael said.

'She is a child of the light, and she will fulfil her purpose.'

'What purpose might that be, Metatron?'

'She is and will be the protector of Heaven, but you also know she can turn to the darkness. She is the child of an Archangel and a human. What were you thinking having a child with a human, Michael?'

'As they continued to argue, I returned to Sarra and Berenike to find Sarra's home destroyed. While I was away from them, Jovan had unleashed his hatred upon her. I ran around what was left of the house. Her home was unrecognisable. I lifted away the debris. When I found her, she was barely alive.'

Sarra opened her eyes as she lay in Michael's arms.

'It was Jovan. He's out of his mind. He tried to kill Berenike. Promise me you'll protect her, Michael. She's too important, keep her safe.'

'I promise, my love.'

Sara's eyes slowly closed. As silence swept over the Archangels, they could feel Michael's heart breaking.

'Something is terribly wrong. I must go to him,' said Gabriel.

Metatron nodded in agreement. Michael placed his hands on her crushed body as he waited patiently for the light to heal her, but there was no light. As he tried repeatedly, his heart was breaking.

Gabriel appeared before his friend to witness the destruction through his own eyes. As he looked around at the devastation, he saw his friend trying desperately to save the woman he loved.

'Gabriel, it's not working.'

'Here, let me try.' Gabriel had the same result. 'I don't understand why it's not working.'

'It's not working because she's gone.' Gabriel placed his hand on his friend's shoulder. 'You know God would not allow this to happen without good reason, Michael.'

As he looked around at the destruction, Gabriel could hear Berenike crying. Gabriel was not only Michael's ally, he was also his friend. He was the only one of the Archangels who understood Michael's love for Sarra.

Gabriel knew of the consequences of a child born from a human and an Archangel. He knew in the wrong hands, Michael's child could be used to do great evil.

Gabriel still could not bring himself to hate Berenike. He helped Michael clear away the debris as he lifted her tenderly into his arms and healed the scratches on her face. Gabriel's heart was breaking for Michael as he realised Jovan had declared war on him.

'I am so very sorry, Michael. I promise you, we will stop him.'

Michael, consumed in his grief, removed Sarra's blackened and burnt body from the debris, then walked to the clearing, where he raised her body above him.

'You fix this! You fix this now!' he screamed to God. 'I have been your servant for an eternity, and I ask this one thing from you. Bring her back now.'

Gabriel knew Michael's request would go unheard.

Michael dropped to his knees, and as he held Sarra in his arms, he whispered, 'Please, Father, bring her back to me.' He could then feel Gabriel's hand on his shoulder.

Jovan's sinister laugh echoed through the ruins of Sarra's home.

'I will come back for your daughter, Michael. She will never be safe. I will be watching as she grows up.' His evil smile burnt right through them both as Gabriel tightened his grip on Berenike.

'Why have you done this, Jovan?' said Michael.

Jovan could see the effects of his actions, and he leaned in close to Michael and said, 'Because I belong on that throne, and I will have my revenge on God. I will reign over the dominion of Earth and its people, and Berenike will be my Queen.'

'My daughter will never stand by your side, Jovan!'

'Sarra died in my arms, and then my child was sent away from me. That was the day I died inside as well,' Michael said. 'All I could hear was my daughter screaming. Sarra's family declared our daughter would one day battle Jovan. She would defeat him. She would have the power of the great High Priestess and be blessed by the hand of God because she was part Archangel. You see, Gaige, my daughter was considered an abomination to those in Heaven.'

'And now?' said Gaige.

'Well, now they seem to be a little more enthusiastic in her presence. Angels are not supposed to have favourites here on Earth. We are from God, and God loves all creatures equally.'

Michael was almost ashamed to say those words, as he had an inherent duty, but of course his love for his child was stronger than any of them above had ever imagined.

'We have all spent several millennia guarding her and keeping her safe from him. She has no idea how powerful she is about to become and how important she is to humanity and Heaven. How important she is to all of us. Even we do not know what to expect. You know, she looks just like her mother, and just as beautiful.'

Gaige could sense the loss of Berenike's mother weighed heavily on him.

'I'm trying to protect her, and she's the one who's going to save the Heavens.' Gaige placed his hand on Michael's shoulder. He couldn't help feeling for him. Michael had missed so much. At that moment, he wasn't an Angel; he was simply her father.

Berenike was listening to everything, and she finally heard the truth. Gabriel was right: her mother's death had broken his heart.

'He really does love me.' Berenike smiled as she called for Michael. 'Father.'

'I'm coming!' he yelled. Michael heard Berenike's cry for help and knew exactly where to look.

CHAPTER TWENTY-THREE

MICHAEL'S LITTLE GIRL

Michael and Gaige found Berenike hiding as they approached in the darkness behind the building. Gaige got to her first. Berenike looked for her father, and as he arrived, she didn't take her eyes off him. Michael looked her over to see how badly she was hurt. She was now looking at him with fresh eyes.

'Gaige, go, I will stay with her. The Archangels need your help. Jovan's numbers are too many. Go and get the others. We will regroup. It's time to work out a plan.'

Gaige bowed at the instruction. He was dismissed like an employee who had just finished his shift, so he decided to leave instead of getting the others and disappeared into the alleyway out of sight. He was furious there was not even a thank you from Michael for being Berenike's protector all those years.

Michael wiped the blood from the scratches on Berenike's face. 'I think your arm's broken, and it looks like just a flesh wound.'

She watched him look her over. He was very gentle with her.

'He stabbed me.' She could see the concern on his face as his eyes moistened and became tears. Berenike gripped her father's arm as she held on to him. 'Don't cry, Father, I'm OK,' she said as she shivered.

'Are you cold?'

'Yes.' Berenike had started shaking from the shock of her wounds.

As Michael drew her close, he cradled her in his arms. His wings became visible as they wrapped around them both.

'I can't properly heal you. Not yet; he'll sense it and find you. Just hold on a little longer.'

As the battle progressed, he sat there cradling his daughter in his arms. Michael sat in silence, listening to the fighting on the streets. They could hear the screams and cries of the people and Angelic creatures, all suffering as they succumbed to their death. The screaming was blood-curdling. The sound of the cries from the street was upsetting. As Michael looked down at his daughter's face as she rested in his arms, he could see how much it was all upsetting her. He began to hum a lullaby; the melody was soothing but very familiar.

'Is that what you used to sing to me as a baby?' she asked as she looked up into his eyes.

'Yes.' He held on tight.

She smiled as she felt for the first time what it was like to have the loving touch of a parent. 'I heard what you said to Gaige,' Berenike said.

He closed his eyes, annoyed. 'I didn't want you to find out like that.'

'I know we haven't really talked about it, but I know what happened now. That's all that matters.'

As she snuggled in closer to his chest, her curiosity got the better of her. 'Tell me about Mother?'

Michael smiled at her request. 'I was wondering when you would ask. Well, you have her strength and curiosity. We could talk for hours about what was out there beyond the veil. You're like her in so many ways, and you have her stubbornness too.'

'I do not,' she whined. They both laughed. 'Was she pretty?'

Her father smiled at her question. 'Berenike, she was beautiful, inside and out, just like you.'

She smiled at him, and he could see Sarra's eyes in his child's face. 'I love you, even if you do get a little cranky at times.'

Her declaration completely melted his heart. To hear those words from his daughter was more than anything he ever could have hoped.

'I love you too, sweetheart.'

They sat quietly as she closed her eyes and fell asleep in her father's arms.

An hour had passed, and Berenike woke to the sound of Michael's voice.

'I think it's safe to heal you now.'

'He's going to kill me, isn't he?' Berenike sat up.

'I won't let him.' Michael was defiant.

'You can't keep protecting me from him. If this is my destiny, to stop him from taking over the Heavens, then you need to have a little faith in me. Michael, you need to stop looking at the situation as my father. You're a soldier who's about to go into battle against the greatest enemy we've ever known. There is way too much at stake here.'

Metatron could hear Berenike's conversation with her father as he approached them.

'I'm not losing you again, Berenike.'

'Haven't you learnt anything from watching me all those years, Father? I will not let him take our home.' Berenike could be very stubborn, as Michael was learning. 'You have to let me try. You have to let me defend the heavens.'

'She's definitely your daughter. She's more like you than you realise, Michael,' Metatron said with a smile.

Before he could utter another word, she took Michael's hand and placed it on her wound. A brilliant light radiated from her entire body as her injuries disappeared within the light. They stood up together and walked to the streets, where they witnessed the destruction of humanity. She could see demons feasting off the bodies of humans and Angels. So many who had lost the battle were lying on the streets where she once lived.

Guardian Angels and other beings of light, relatives who had passed away, neighbours and friends she'd once known in her neighbourhood, and those who had crossed over to either Heaven or Hell, all just scattered within the destruction.

As she walked down the middle of the street watching the fighting, the destruction around her was devastating. Her beloved Earth was ruined.

The tears rolling down her face showed her skin layered in ash as she witnessed the conflict between Heaven, Earth and Hell. The sight of teenagers and children picking up what they could find to arm themselves against the evil that was taking over. Humanity was fighting back, side by side with the Archangels, for humanity and Heaven.

Berenike felt her heart torn in several different directions. As she separated from her father and the group, she continued to look at her surroundings. She could see the state of the buildings surrounding her store; the damage would take months to fix. The leaves on the trees and flowers that blossomed with the change of the seasons had all wilted from the fire that had now set upon most of the surrounding buildings. She saw the fear in the eyes of the children who had taken up arms.

'How am I going to fix this? So many dead?'

'Do you see what you've done?' asked Jovan as he crept towards her from behind. 'You can stop all of this right now. You can stop all this destruction. You can save your friends and all the people you care for.'

She could feel his breath on her neck. His words became more intoxicating by the minute.

'This is all because of you.' He raised his voice impatiently.

Berenike glanced over to see Michael fighting alongside Gabriel as they cornered several demons. Amy, EJ, and Raphael all worked as a team to defend the children who were running and screaming in fear. Her heart was breaking.

'Their fate is in your hands, Berenike. It's all up to you.'

'What do I have to do?' she asked, defeated.

'Say yes. Say that you'll be by my side in my Kingdom, and it all stops.'

'Yes.'

No sooner had she said yes, Jovan took on his evil, grotesque form. As he grasped Berenike by the throat, his long, twisted fingers wrapped entirely around her neck as if it were a perfect fit. His damaged wings wrapped around her like a spider trapping its prey in its web, unable to escape.

As her tears fell, her eyes caught Michael's glance as she whispered, 'I love you.'

CHAPTER TWENTY-FOUR

PRISONER OF WAR

Jovan had taken Berenike to Hell. As they entered his throne room, he threw her to the floor and sat down on his throne.

'Tie her hands and keep an eye on her,' he said to his henchmen.

As did Jovan, they could sense the light within her. As the beings of Hell surrounded her, they could all sense that essence of goodness and the light that would bring the salvation that had eluded them for an eternity.

'Away from her!' Jovan raised his hand to remove his followers.

'Sire, why did you bring her here? Why didn't you just take her to Heaven and destroy him?' asked Minion.

'Because I haven't decided what I'm going to do with her yet!' he yelled. 'Soon, but not yet.' Jovan rose off his throne and stood in front of Berenike. 'I am sorry it has come to this.'

'I thought I was your guest?' she said to him spitefully.

'I changed my mind. Now you're my prisoner,' he said with a grin.

'Do you honestly think you can take the Kingdom of God? Talk about delusions of grandeur,' she said as she laughed at him.

'Your father is the reason I'm not on my throne.'

She laughed. 'Seriously, grow up. I've met six-year-olds more mature than you, Jovan. You betrayed my father, and you killed my mother. You were banished to this place because you betrayed who you were as an Archangel and everything it stands for.' He moved closer to her, and she could feel his seductive presence. 'I will never join you.'

'You will be by my side,' he said to her forcefully. 'If you say yes to being my Queen and sit beside me in my Kingdom, it will be easier for you.'

She looked deep into his eyes and could see the Archangel trapped within him. She could see his soul trapped deep within the darkness of his dark eyes. For a moment, she could still see him as an Archangel. She could feel his breath on her cheek as he pressed his body against hers forcefully. His seductions were overwhelming as his lips caressed hers. Berenike had to keep her focus and not be seduced by his overwhelming masculinity.

'Say yes, and we can have anything we want. Together, be anyone we want. There will be no restrictions to who you are. I can give you everything you have ever dreamed of. We will make a great team. Just say yes.' As he held her in his arms, and he waited for her answer.

'Jovan,' she said.

'Yes.' The anticipation of the situation was exciting him as he held her in his arms.

'I'd rather eat mud than be by your side,' she said coldly.

Jovan released his grip on her and quietly stepped away. She could feel his anger growing. 'Well, that's unfortunate for you.' he said.

Berenike was scared. She could feel something was about to erupt in him. She remembered what Gabriel had said to her: when she needed him, she was to call for him.

'Gabriel.'

Just as Berenike spoke his name, he heard her words. 'Berenike!' he screamed. 'He's taken her to Hell. She's in trouble.'

Jovan thrust his hand into her chest. She was screaming as her body began to shake; the pain was unfathomable.

Michael heard Berenike's scream throughout the Heavens. 'He's killing her! We must hurry.'

Throughout the Heavens, Berenike's blood-curdling scream echoed. She could feel her life diminishing as Jovan fed off the light of God within her. If she wouldn't go to him of her own free will, he would take her light any way he could.

Each Archangel leapt into action to save Berenike. Gaige's disappearance during the fighting on Earth had played on Gabriel's mind. Amy's words were ringing in his ears. He agreed he needed to keep an eye on him, especially where Berenike was concerned. As he mysteriously appeared in Hell, Gabriel thought it was odd.

As they all entered the underworld to find them, Michael and Gaige headed for Jovan's throne room. Michael was frantic with worry for his daughter.

As they entered the throne room, he could see Berenike's life literally draining before his eyes.

'No!' he screamed as he ran towards them.

Jovan saw Michael and smirked. He was no longer in his human form. The grotesque side of his hatred had transformed him into a twisted being of darkness. His skin was grey, his eyes dark.

He had teeth that would cut like a razor, and the energy radiating off his body was of pure hate. It made Michael physically sick.

Gaige ran to Berenike's side; she was unconscious. For the moment, there was nothing he could do for her. He looked over at Michael, who was battling the demon. Gaige then decided to attack Jovan from the other side. As they were battling Jovan, the other Archangels appeared. As Metatron, Raphael, and Uriel all defended their brother, fighting side by side, Gabriel ran to Berenike, lifted her into his arms, and they disappeared.

CHAPTER TWENTY-FIVE

OLD FRIENDS

Michael was furious that his daughter had been hurt again. He knew the situation was grim; Berenike's injuries were worse than her last encounter with Jovan, but the fact that she was with Gabriel; Michael knew he would protect her.

Jovan was seething as he swung his sword.

'How dare you touch my daughter!' said Michael.

Michael was furious that such evil had dared touch a child of God's light. More so because she was *his* child.

Michael stood strong as he attacked Jovan. He wouldn't stop until the result was final.

'Brother, do you honestly think you can stop me?'

Jovan was psychologically clever. He knew how to play on emotions.

'We are not brothers.'

Michael was full of anger. Jovan had stepped over the line by harming his daughter. As Michael and Jovan fought hard, the

Archangels battled the evil beings that had occupied Hell through the eons of time. They were the fallen. Those that had sided with Jovan during his last attempt at a takeover of the Heavens. The souls that betrayed God.

Metatron and Michael had Jovan cornered when they could see the throne room was filling with the enemy.

'Join me, Michael. We can forget the past and start again. You can join my army, and Berenike can be my Queen. She'll rule the Heavens with me.'

His words made Michael angry. Metatron and Raphael continued to corner him. Just as Michael raised his sword to strike, Jovan's words were completely unexpected.

'You know the prophecy, Michael. You know from the child of light will come a being of great darkness and evil. You know it will happen. You know she will give birth to the future King of Hell.'

'What is he talking about, Michael?' Metatron asked.

'He hasn't told you everything about the prophecy, Metatron.' Jovan had now created doubt in Metatron's mind.

'The prophecy has nothing to do with Berenike. The prophecy was about you, Jovan. You were the child of God's light, and you are the one that turned to darkness. If she does happen to bear a child, they will be good and of God. There is absolutely no way that will happen.'

'That's right,' said Raphael. 'We will all be in the child's life. It will be impossible for them to turn to darkness.' His laugh echoed throughout hell.

'Raphael, you're such a sheep,' said Jovan.

'Join me now. Lay down your sword. It is your last chance,' he said to Michael.

'Never. The Kingdom of God will never fall to you. You're a failure, Jovan.'

Michael swung his sword at Jovan as the Archangels all went into attack formation. Jovan was outnumbered, and they fought him and his legion to the point of exhaustion.

'Retreat.'

Michael and the others all fled Jovan's throne room and headed back to Heaven. He knew Berenike was with Gabriel, and that at least gave him some peace, even though he remained nervous at the fact that she wasn't within his eyes' reach.

CHAPTER TWENTY-SIX

GABRIEL'S LOVE

Gabriel had taken Berenike back to her house, relieved now that she was in his arms. He wasn't sure if they would look for them there, but for the moment they were safe.

Still unconscious, he placed her on the lounge. He could see her wounds were deep and bloody, and he tore apart the bathroom cabinet for anything he could find to clean her wounds. As he entered the lounge room, he saw Berenike had awakened and was trying to get up off the lounge to leave.

'Are you crazy?!' he yelled. 'You need to lie down!'

'Gabriel, I have to go back to them. I have to help them.'

She could barely speak. She was badly injured. It became apparent she was going to try to leave, but Gabriel was adamant it wasn't going to happen. As she wrestled with him, her energy was disappearing. She was growing weaker by the minute and could barely stand.

'Let me go.' Berenike couldn't fight anymore, and she weakened as she cried in his arms.

Gabriel realised everything that had happened up until that point had finally caught up with her. She'd been so strong for such a long time. He held her in his arms as she cried. Her tears overwhelmed him, and his heart

was breaking for her. Since Berenike's arrival in Heaven, Gabriel had struggled with his emotions towards her.

He stroked her hair and ran his fingers over her cheeks to remove her tears. He kissed her, and she didn't fight him. He loved her beyond words. She was no longer the child he'd watched and protected from afar. During the years, he'd seen the woman she'd grown into. His kiss was a long time coming.

'Sit down so I can clean your wounds. It looks bad.'

She sat down and watched him as he tended to her injuries. They both quietly sat before each other without speaking. As the minutes went by, she started to smile. He smiled back at her.

'You've wanted to do that for a while, haven't you?' she said.

'I'm glad you noticed,' he said with a degree of shyness. He inspected her wounds but found it difficult to see how bad it really was. 'I can't see how bad your wound is.'

She began to remove her clothing with some degree of difficulty. 'You'll have to help me take it off,' she said. 'Normally, this is the part where you've already bought me a drink.'

They both laughed, then Gabriel helped her remove her bloodstained bodice so he could dress the wound and stop the bleeding. As she cried out from the pain, Gabriel was shocked at what he saw. Jovan had managed to take a huge chunk out of Berenike's chest where he'd tried to take the light from within her.

She leaned forward, placing her head against his chest as he wiped the blood from her back. The closer she was to him, the safer she felt. He could feel her lips and breath on his neck. He couldn't resist her, kissing her as the warmth of his hands ran across her back and shoulders.

'Not here,' she said as she stared into his loving eyes.

'I have loved you almost my entire existence. Losing you would be too much to bear, dear one. You must be more careful,' he said, cradling her cheek in his hand.

He knew his love for her would cloud his judgement. She was without a doubt his greatest weakness but also his best strength. She sat quietly for a moment as he helped her get dressed. Gabriel knew they had both finally given in to their feelings for one another, and he welcomed it.

'We'll talk when this is all over.' Berenike nodded in agreement. 'Do you have any more bandages?'

'Yes, they should be in the bathroom unless Amy's cleaned it all out by now,' she said as he got up to get more supplies.

Gabriel sorted through the bathroom cabinet, trying to find anything he could use to stop the bleeding. He knew he needed to heal her, and it became more apparent that nothing on Earth was going to fix a part-human, part-Archangel. Her wounds were too deep.

As he entered the lounge room, he could see she was in pain. She was becoming weaker by the minute. Gabriel lifted her into his arms, and he could feel her relax as she put her arms around his neck and held on tight.

'I'm taking you home so I can heal you there,' he said.

Gabriel moved swiftly as they flew back into Heaven. He took her back to his room, removed her bloodstained clothing, and bathed her wounds. As he took a deep breath, he wasn't about to let his nerves get the better of him. The last person Gabriel tried to heal was Berenike's mother. When he failed, he lost faith in himself and never attempted to heal anyone again. Berenike was too important to him, and he was not going to fail this time.

He placed his hands over her chest wound and closed his eyes. Just as Berenike had manifested her sword, Gabriel was able to heal her from the light from God. The Archangels all had healing abilities, but Gabriel hadn't used his for such a long time. He would move the Heavens to get her well again. He stood as tall as the most brilliant light shone throughout the room. It was spectacular and brought his love back to life again. Her wound had disappeared within the light; Gabriel had healed her.

Gabriel removed his battle uniform. Berenike's blood had covered his chest plating and armour, so he washed her blood from his skin, then observed her as she slept soundly. Being near her gave him a sense of peace. Deciding to leave her to rest to get her strength back, he kissed her cheek and walked out onto his balcony to check on the Heavens as he basked in the rays of God. Gabriel was concerned that Jovan would bring the fight to the heavens. He knew it was only a matter of time.

Berenike opened her eyes and could see Gabriel in the distance. She ran her hand over her chest where her wounds used to be. She smiled to herself, then got up out of bed, wrapped the sheet around her body, and walked out onto the balcony to join him. She slid her arms around his waist as her cheek rested on his back. He smiled, holding her hands close to his chest.

'Thank you,' she whispered.

'I'm glad you're awake. You had me worried. Come inside with me.' He directed her back into his room so they could have their much-needed talk.

As Gabriel began to speak, she quieted him with a 'Shhh.' He held her in his arms, and her skin began to tingle. He kissed her as the sheet that covered her body fell to the ground. Berenike stood there naked in his arms. She didn't care that she was exposed before him; she was completely in love with him. He'd saved her life, and now she couldn't imagine her existence without him. He kissed her again, and she responded to his touch. He lowered her body to the bed, and his lips caressed her neck. His muscular body glistened gold in the candle light that lit up the room. She ran her hands over every inch of his skin; his touch was both sensual and loving. His fingers and breath lingered over her body and completely set her on fire. She'd never experienced lovemaking in the way she did with Gabriel. That was the difference; he was all love, and she was completely his, mind, body, and soul. Gabriel now had the freedom to express how he felt for her. His sensual touch and the passion within his kisses had her craving him more and more. She gripped his shoulders with her nails as the urgency of her body made them both quiver while she shook beneath him. They made love several times that night.

As he held her in his arms, Gabriel found the courage to speak. 'I'm sorry I lost you. When I couldn't find you, I panicked.'

She smiled at his declaration. 'Do you have any idea how much I love you?' she whispered.

He kissed her tenderly. To her, he was perfect. He was the perfect lover and best friend all rolled into one. Finally being able to express his love for her and have Berenike return those feelings was something Gabriel had only ever dreamed of.

'I can see the light in your eyes when you smile, dear one.'

Berenike could see Gabriel's wings tucked in behind his back. She reached over his shoulder to touch his wing. As an Archangel, they were an important part of his being. Her fingers touched his feathers and sent a shiver through his body.

'I had no idea they would be as soft as this.'

'They're as soft as your hair,' he said to her as he ran his fingers through the length of her hair. Everything felt different in Heaven, and his feathers were as soft as velvet.

'Promise me you won't hide them from me. They're too beautiful to hide. I wish I had wings,' she said to him, still stroking his feathers.

Gabriel's wing traveled over his shoulder and tickled her back as she giggled. No being had ever complemented Gabriel on his wings before, but Berenike really did love them.

As he ran his fingers down her chest where her wound use to be, Berenike sat up next to him, her expression saddened.

'What is it?'

'He's still coming for me, Gabriel, I'm scared I won't be strong enough to stop him. You know, I could still see the Angel in him when I spoke to him. It's like he's trapped in there. I honestly didn't think he would hurt me, but I was so wrong. The Archangel in him is still in there. I've seen it, but it's struggling to get to the surface,' she said as Gabriel listened.

He was starting to believe Berenike just might be able to bring Jovan back to the light. 'I've never known you to fear anything. You're one of the most fearless souls I've ever known. It's one of the things I love about you. The light within you is from God, so with what you have inherited of your mother's abilities as well means you can manifest the light to stop him. We still are not aware of how you will use it, but it is there within you. It is a part of you. We just should wait for the right moment. I will be there by your side, Berenike. You don't have to do this on your own. In fact, I insist on being there with you,' he said forcefully.

Berenike smiled at him, and as they lay in each other's arms, they could hear the others had arrived back in Heaven.

Uriel burst through the bedroom door to find the two of them together. 'Hurry, your father is on his way,' he said.

Berenike was startled to see him standing before her, considering they were still in bed together. Uriel couldn't look at her; he blushed at seeing them together.

'Uriel, we really need to have a chat about the use of doors,' Berenike said.

Gabriel laughed. 'It's all right. Uriel knows how much I love you. He's known for a while now.'

Berenike didn't care that Uriel knew. It was a relief she didn't have to keep secrets around him, but she was more nervous about her father finding out.

They both got out of bed and dressed.

'Thank you, friend,' Gabriel said to Uriel as they left the room.

CHAPTER TWENTY-SEVEN

THANK YOU

Berenike was nervous as she left the room with Gabriel at her side. Gabriel took a deep breath as he saw Michael approaching in the distance. Michael's eyes looked for his daughter. As he saw Berenike standing there, he started to run, and she ran as fast as she could into her father's arms. He pulled her in close to his chest and held her as he cried. He thought he'd seen the last of her as he battled Jovan.

'I thought you were dead. Lord, thank you for watching over my daughter,' he said as he held Berenike as tightly as he could.

'Actually, I'd be dead right now if it wasn't for Gabriel. He healed me.' She lovingly looked over at Gabriel and smiled.

'Gabriel, you have not healed anyone in over a thousand years,' Michael said, shocked at Gabriel's gesture.

Metatron smiled to himself. He was an Angel of few words, but he was very observant.

'A thousand years? You did that for me?' Berenike said to Gabriel.

He nodded. He really did love her.

Michael placed his hand on Gabriel's shoulder. 'Thank you, my friend.'

'Berenike, we've been discussing a battle plan. We all know he is coming for you. Probably more so now that you got away from him,' said Metatron.

'Metatron, Earth is in ruins. Most of it is unrecognisable, and it's all because of me. I can't allow Jovan to keep doing this. Human beings are capable of many things, of great atrocities, but they don't deserve this! This is not part of their world; they don't have the ability to fight like us. They don't know how to. They don't know why he wants Heaven. This isn't their fight, so it's up to us to fight for them.'

'What do you propose, child?'

'He wants a fight, so give him what he wants. Let's draw him out.'

'No, it's too dangerous,' said Uriel.

'Berenike, if we do this, there's a good chance some of us won't survive - and if you fail, we'll lose Heaven,' said Michael.

'I won't fail, Father. I'm not losing my family. This is my home now,' Berenike said as she looked at each of them.

Uriel grinned. Raphael stood tall with his chest robust while Metatron basked in her statement. She was right. They were a family now. They all cared for her, but the battle for Heaven would unite them in ways that would make the bond between them stronger than before. She considered them all her family, and she knew they would protect her until the end of time.

Gabriel remained quiet, but Berenike could see the worry on his face. 'I never thought I'd say this, but I need more training. All right, team, we've got work to do,' she said.

Raphael, Uriel, and Metatron all followed her as she headed for the training room. Michael stayed back to talk to Gabriel.

'Gabriel, not so fast. I think we need to talk.' This was the moment Gabriel was dreading as he faced Michael. 'What's going on between you and my daughter?'

'I'm not sure how to answer your question, Michael,' Gabriel responded, nervous.

'Sure you are, Gabriel.' Gabriel remained silent. 'All right, then, answer me this: are you in love with her?'

Gabriel looked Michael in the eye as he spoke. 'I love her with every part of who I am. I would die for her so she could take just one more breath. Yes, Michael, I'm in love with your daughter.'

Having confirmed Michael's suspicions, Gabriel bowed his head and left the room to join the others. As he entered the combat room, he glanced over at Berenike. She could see the look on his face and knew straight away her father knew about the two of them. Michael followed Gabriel and stood there, watching them all work together. He said nothing to them as he left the room.

They all went through their combat techniques, practicing different scenarios and outcomes of battle.

'I'm going to talk to Father about us,' Berenike said, waiting for Gabriel to give her his approval.

'Do you think that's wise? He hasn't said anything to me in hours.' Gabriel finally said, 'I think he's upset with me.'

He was worried. He loved Berenike, but he also loved Michael like a brother. Being his friend also made the situation more difficult.

'I'll go and find him,' Berenike said, then kissed Gabriel goodbye and went to look for her father.

CHAPTER TWENTY-EIGHT

LOSS AND ACCEPTANCE

Berenike looked everywhere for her father in Heaven. She searched the grounds and even flew into the light to try to locate him, and it was in that moment she realised she knew where to look. She found Michael where he'd buried Sarra; his special and sacred place. As she flew in, she could see him seated and staring straight ahead into the horizon. She knew this would be a difficult conversation.

She approached her father and sat down next to him on the seat. As they sat in silence, she reached for his hand to hold. 'Gabriel told you, didn't he?' she asked.

'He told me he would die for you. He loves you,' Michael said as he faced his daughter. Berenike could see he wasn't happy. 'He loves you the same way I loved your mother.

Her father's confirmation of Gabriel's feelings for her brought a tear to Berenike's eye. 'I love him too, Father, more than I've ever loved any man, but you know you'll always be the most important man in my life, don't you? You're my father, and nothing will ever change that. You know I love you too, right?'

'I only just got you back, and now...' Michael choked on his words as he tried to speak.

'I'm not going anywhere. I'll always be yours, first and foremost,' Berenike said as she hugged him. 'I am so blessed that you love me as much as you do. I'm not going anywhere from you. I'm home now. I'm finally home.'

Michael sat quietly with his arms around his daughter.

'I wasn't looking for it, Father. It just happened. I didn't expect to fall in love. I never dreamed I'd meet anyone like Gabriel. I never believed anyone would love me as deeply as he does, except you of course.' Michael sighed heavily as he listened to his daughter's words. 'I have to admit, you're not reacting in the way I thought you would. You haven't tried to kill him yet,' Berenike said, trying to lighten the mood. They both laughed at the comment. 'On Earth, that's pretty much common practice between fathers and daughters when a new man comes into her life.' She laughed, trying to lighten the mood.

'That's because I know it's real between the two of you. He healed you. He hasn't done that in a very long time, Berenike,' Michael said. 'Gabriel is my friend, and I'm very grateful he saved my daughter's life. I cannot hate him. I've been watching you both for a while now. Seeing you together, it reminds me of your mother and me. How happy we were. Because of that, I have a good idea of how much he loves you. Never doubt how he feels about you. I've never seen Gabriel like this. He's been in love with you all these years.' He stroked her hair as he wiped the tears from her eyes, then shook his head in disbelief. 'I can't believe I missed it.' As Michael laughed to himself, Berenike realised how much of what he'd just said to her was from his heart. 'It's times like these I miss your mother. She should be here to talk to you.'

Berenike smiled. The bond she'd now formed with her father was strong. In the many months she'd been in Heaven, she knew he would die for her without hesitation.

'I think you're doing just fine,' she reassured him.

As they sat quietly, Gabriel appeared before them, and Michael stood up to confront his friend. While Gabriel realized he would have to endure Michael's anger, Michael could feel Gabriel's heart the moment he saw Berenike; she smiled at the sight of him. No matter how hard he tried, Michael knew it was pointless to be angry.

He looked Gabriel in the eye and said, 'Your duty to Heaven must always come first. Your relationship with Berenike can never get in the way. Do you hear me?!'

'Yes, Michael.'

As Gabriel turned to walk away, Michael moved in close to him, and Gabriel could feel his breath on his face as he spoke. 'And if you ever hurt her, I'll take your wings!'

'Please forgive me, Michael. I love her,' Gabriel said as he looked Michael in the eye.

As Michael fought back tears, he placed his hand on Gabriel's shoulder. 'I know, friend.'

As Michael disappeared, Gabriel and Berenike both stood before each other.

'Does this mean what I think it does?'

She smiled. Her heart was full of love for him. God had been good to her. He gave her a father, a love, and a new family. She felt blessed indeed.

CHAPTER TWENTY-NINE

THE TRAP

As things were quiet on Earth for the moment, Berenike and the Archangels decided to devise the best strategy to capture Jovan.

'It's risky, Berenike, but if we hit him all at once, he won't have any other choice but to come after you,' said Metatron. 'We will set about attacking Hell to draw him out, then he's all yours.'

Uriel was worried, very quiet as he stood with the others. Berenike noticed his lack of response.

'It's going to be OK, you know,' she said to him.

She placed her hand on his to reassure him, but he withdrew his hand from hers. He, along with the other Archangels, had all developed a bond with her now that wouldn't easily be broken, but Uriel was concerned. He didn't approve of her being the bait. The greatest bond, however, was the strength they all shared as one.

'We are all with you, child,' Raphael said.

Berenike could tell he was proud of her, and she embraced him. 'Thank you, Raph,' she said as they all smiled.

'All right, so we all know the plan?' Michael asked as everyone nodded in agreement. 'Let's go.'

Uriel was hesitant to leave Berenike's side.

'I know you don't approve of this, but there's no other way. We need to surprise him. He won't be expecting us, so it's the perfect opportunity,' she told him.

Berenike grasped Uriel's hand so he couldn't leave. They all loved her, but she now filled a special place in Uriel's heart. He was extremely fond of her, having watched her grow into the warrior they all knew was emerging before them.

Uriel kissed her forehead, then left. As they all left the combat room, Berenike could sense the worry in Gabriel.

'Stop worrying, OK? I'm going to be fine,' he told her, then pulled her in close to his chest and kissed her. 'I don't need to tell you to call for me if you need me, do I?'

'Keep kissing me like that, and I'll never stop calling for you,' she said, smiling.

Gabriel's lack of conversation showed how concerned he was for Berenike. She could see the panic in his eyes.

'Let's go save our home, Gabriel. I can do this, and just maybe I can save him as well,' she said.

She took his hand as they travelled to Hell. As they all took their places strategically, Berenike stood in the middle of the throne room as she called for Jovan. Since he was attracted to the light of God, she decided the best way to entice him was to fill the room with light. She lit up the throne room and used herself as bait - and like a moth to a flame, he appeared.

Jovan appeared before them, seated on his throne.

'Minion, we have guests,' Jovan yelled.

Minion appeared beside his King. His constant loyalty to Jovan was unwavering. 'Oh look, it's a family reunion,' said Minion, laughing hysterically.

'Berenike, you're alive. What a surprise. In fact, I'd say you're positively glowing.' Jovan laughed as he looked over at Gabriel. 'Now, that's something I didn't expect,' he said as he surveyed them both.

Gabriel territorially moved closer to stand beside Berenike. He wasn't about to let him hurt her again.

'So, Michael, if I'd have known you were coming to visit, I would have put on brunch. I'd offer you a drink, but I don't want to.'

'Enough!' yelled Michael. 'Berenike, now!'

Just as they'd taken position, Berenike let off a beam of her light, which knocked Jovan flying off his throne. She was angry at his attempted destruction of her beloved Earth and set off an attack of her own on the surroundings of his throne room. As she began to set off beam after beam of light, the building where they stood began to crumble around them. Minion scrambled to take cover.

'What do you think you're doing, Berenike?' Jovan demanded. His fury at her defiance of his commands was showing.

'How do you like it? Have a taste of your own medicine,' Berenike yelled. She set off the destruction of the underworld, her rage beginning to fill the room. 'And this one's for my mother!' She targeted the beam of light at Jovan's throne, which went flying and fell on top of him.

'Stop them!' Jovan yelled.

His henchmen surrounded the Archangels and moved in closer towards them as they filled the room. They all began to fight, blade after blade clashing as good and evil challenged each other. As the numbers dwindled, Jovan's focus remained on Berenike. He ran straight to her, gripped her by the hair, and disappeared with her. Michael's eyes widened as he watched Berenike disappear with Jovan.

'Retreat!' he yelled. 'We know where he's taking her. Everyone back to the Heavens, now!'

Jovan decided it was time. He finally had Berenike where he wanted her, alone with him, and he could now force her to kill God and take control of the Heavens.

As they both entered the Heavenly Palace, he weaved his way through to the different levels of Heaven. He'd already planted some of his followers in the palace, and Berenike could see bodies everywhere as he dragged her through each level of the palace. While her father and the Archangels were on their way back to heaven, Jovan was wreaking havoc on each level of Heaven.

'Jovan, you don't have to do this. He'll forgive you. Just stop what you're doing.' Jovan threw her toward a set of stairs, but she continued. 'You were once one of them. They're your family. Come home.'

'No!' he yelled as he struck her across the face.

The impact of Jovan's assault had Berenike reeling across the room again, and she felt the pain from his assault; he'd left her face bruised and bleeding. She stood up and managed to run, making her way up the stairs to the top level of Heaven. She'd never been this far into the palace before. To the human eye, it looked like she'd been traveling up a set of spiral stairs, winding as she proceeded further and further.

As Berenike passed from floor to floor, on each level she saw the results of Jovan's evil. Everywhere she looked, she saw bodies. These were the guardians of the Seven Heavens, warriors who would protect each realm. Her heart was breaking as she observed the many faces of each soul that lay before her; Jovan had been strategic in planning an assault on each level of Heaven.

She reached the entrance to God's throne room. At the doorway, she saw a being of light draped in a brilliant white robe who radiated love towards Berenike and held out her hand to her.

'No!' Berenike screamed.

She recognised the being; it was the same Angel who had taken her hand and led her further into the rays of God's light when she explored Heaven. Berenike nursed the being in her arms and cradled her as the Angel took her last breath.

'Stop him!' said the spirit before her, then its life slowly vanished before her eyes and turned to dust.

As Berenike reached the Seventh Heaven, she found a huge staircase with a red carpet leading to the top. She made her way up the many stairs, then, hurt and trembling, she stepped through the entrance to what she could see was a room with no doors, white with walls that would rise as high as the clouds above. She drew back the curtains and stepped into the highest level of heaven, the level before God himself.

All of Heaven was quiet. As God stood watching from the Seventh Heaven, he knew it was only a matter of time before

Jovan would join him in the throne room. Berenike had an uneasy feeling of what was awaiting her. She stepped through the doorway and into the light, and before her eyes were two gold thrones. She was seeing it all for the first time. For centuries, humanity had written of God and Heaven without really knowing of its existence, and now Berenike was seeing it all before her eyes. One of the thrones sat on a different level than the other. As she moved closer towards them, her surroundings all became clear.

She was about to appear before God himself. She could barely stand. Jovan's assault on her was violent, as it had always been. As the gold from the thrones shone brightly, they radiated beams of light from where they sat. Berenike flinched at the brightness of the light. She reached out her hand to touch it, and the emotion she felt from what was before her was overwhelming. She swallowed hard as she sensed she wasn't alone. As she looked around the room, she could see a man standing before her, with piercing blue eyes and a face of pure love.

'Hello, Berenike,' said God.

'Hello.'

'We don't have much time, child.'

'I know he's coming.'

'No, he's here,' said Jovan. As he appeared before God, Berenike stepped in front of God to protect him from Jovan.

'How did you get in here? This place has been off limits to you since the day I banished you from my Kingdom.' God was surprised at Jovan's courage, not to mention his ego.

'Hello, Father!' Jobs said mockingly. Berenike could feel the hate in his words. 'Did you honestly think I would forget the way upstairs? Oh, your guardians are dead. They lacked the courage and skills. They have no honour.' God watched Jovan closely as he circled around them both like an animal waiting to pounce on its prey. 'Michael's really let things slide, hasn't he? That's all right. I'll. sort him out.'

'How dare you speak of my father like that!?' Berenike yelled. 'Michael and the others have had to clean up the mess you made from your actions. You're a spoilt child, Jovan, and I will stop you.'

'Berenike, what of the guardians?' God asked her.

'He's killed them at each doorway, all dead,' she said softly. As she stood strong against Jovan, she found her courage. 'You're a coward, Jovan,' she said to him.

'Berenike, join me, and together we can command the Heavens, to rule over eternity and all that is. Take the place of your mother and stand with me, side by side.'

'My mother's place was never with you, Jovan, and neither is mine,' Berenike snapped. She could see how angry Jovan was becoming. 'You're insane. Put down your sword, Jovan. This is your last chance.' She then turned around to face God, raised her hand, and a force field appeared before him, separating them from one another. 'It's for your own protection. Please trust me.'

As God nodded at her request, the Archangels appeared. Gabriel ran towards her, and she raised her hand and created what seemed to be another force field to separate her from those she loved. She shook her head at him; she had to fight Jovan on her own.

'Berenike!' screamed Gabriel. He was frantic.

Both Michael and Gabriel tried to break the force field she'd set up, their fists pounding the energy field before them. With everybody wanting to protect her, Berenike was the one protecting her family.

'Berenike, no!' screamed Gabriel.

Jovan was now standing in front of her. They'd all been waiting for this moment. As Jovan raised his hand to her, a beam of dark light shot out towards her. She countered his attack with the angelic light of God, which sent him flying across the room. Her light was far stronger than he'd ever imagined, and she knew how to use it now; her strength came from the Heavens.

Jovan got up as she approached him, then reached out with his grotesque hand, wrapped his long fingers around her throat, and began to squeeze. Berenike gasped for air. Just as she felt her breath slipping away, a bright flash of light appeared within the throne room.

'Take your hands off my daughter!' yelled Sarra.

'Oh no!' Michael screamed. He was beating his fists against the wall, desperately trying to bring it down. All he could do was stand there and watch as the two people he loved the most faced the worst being in the universe.

Sarra's appearance shocked Jovan to the point where it caught him off guard, and Berenike punched him, then fell to the floor. She got up and ran to her mother's side.

'Hi.'

'My darling, are you all right?' asked Sarra. Berenike nodded yes. 'Stand with me, and we can defeat him together.'

As Sarra began to call on the energy of the Universe, Berenike could hear a voice calling to her.

'Berenike, you know what to do. The light from Heaven will always guide you, even in the darkness. It is within you. Always come from love,' the voice said to her.

Just as Sarra raised her hand to destroy Jovan for the last time, Berenike jumped in front of him to protect him. She then raised her hand to her mother to stop. Next, everyone watched as Berenike used her light to remove the evil within Jovan. The brightness was blinding, and they all squinted from the light. Berenike projected love, just as God had suggested, and the darkness that had occupied Jovan's soul was now removed. As the evil left his body, he screamed, feeling the hate that had occupied his soul for centuries being ripped from within him. The most beautiful light followed as it shone from within his body, and Jovan gasped for air as his lungs filled with life. The Morning Star had returned, and Jovan was reduced to tears as he remembered all he'd done.

Berenike turned to face her mother. 'I won't let you do that, Mother,' she said, remaining defiant.

'Berenike, get out of the way. I won't say it again,' said Sarra.

'You can't replace one hate with another. Getting back at him for what he did by taking his life isn't going to change anything. You must forgive him. Don't you get it? We can all start again if you can forgive.' Sarra was hesitant, but she knew her daughter was right. 'Mother, we're not like any other race, you and I. We're unique, you know that. The way we love, that's beyond anything Earthly.'

Berenike could see the pain in her mother's eyes, which began to show the tears of an emotional separation from her child; a pain that only now could be healed.

'You'll have to get through me to get to him. Are you prepared to do that, Mother? Jovan is an Archangel now. He is of God.'

Berenike stood firm against Sarra, and in Sarra's retreat, she looked to Michael for guidance. He nodded; he could see Berenike would defend him if she had to.

Although Jovan was beaten, to look at him now, Berenike could see why he was known as the Morning Star. He was very beautiful, and his wings were magnificent. His glow was like that of Berenike. She'd cast out the evil that had become second nature to him for several millennia, and he was once again a spiritual being.

Berenike had saved him, just as she said she would. The darkness that had resided in him was now gone.

'He's of the light now, Mother,' Berenike said, standing firm as she knelt in front of Jovan.

'I didn't mean to kill your mother,' Jovan said, full of remorse as his tears began to flow. 'All those years, I've kept you away from your father. I'm so sorry.'

'I know. I forgive you,' Berenike said as she kissed him on the forehead.

He pressed his hand against her stomach and received the immediate flash of a vision. Uriel saw exactly what Jovan was seeing.

Berenike withdrew the wall she'd placed around God and the others.

'Lord, I'll ask only one thing of you: I ask that you let me decide his fate.'

'Granted, child,' God said, curious to see what she'd do next.

They all stood there in silence, Michael standing beside Sarra as they watched their daughter be both judge and jury to the being that had caused so much pain in their world.

'Are you going to kill me?' Jovan asked. 'I deserve to die for what I've done.'

Berenike could see he was scared as he trembled in front of her. 'No, but I am going to do something with the hope that you understand humanity a lot better. I'm going to give you the one thing you've always wanted: I hereby strip all your powers and access to Heaven. You'll have all your memories of your past existence, and you'll remember all the pain you've caused. You'll live as a human being on Earth and experience all that's human. I hope at some point, Jovan, you can redeem yourself from all the wrong you've done. Do you have anything to say?' She waited and watched him hesitate before he spoke.

'Yes.' Jovan stood up, walked close to her, and whispered in her ear, 'You're pregnant,' then kissed her on the cheek. He then stood before God and the Archangels, faced Michael, and said, 'Please forgive me for what I've done.' With a heavy heart, he turned to God and went down on bended knee. 'I am sorry, Father.'

Berenike placed her hands on Jovan's head, and a brilliant light blinded them all as she transformed him into a human, then sent him to Earth.

Amy was at Berenike's house when she heard a huge thud in the lounge room. She could hear Muffin growling from the other room, and as she investigated the noise, she found Jovan on the lounge room floor.

Berenike looked God in the eye, making sure everyone could hear what she had to say. 'Amy, can you hear me?' she said.

Amy was so startled by Berenike's call to her, she dropped her coffee cup on the floor. 'Berenike?!' yelled Amy. 'What is this, the Angel hotline?' Berenike had sent Jovan to her and EJ.

'I want you to let Jovan work in the store. He can stay at my place. Look after him for me. He's human now.'

Amy was hesitant but agreed. She could see Jovan was different now; he was fragile and scared.

'The light has gone out for too many today. I won't take his as well. Jovan is under my protection.'

Seeing Berenike stand strong, Michael reached out his hand to her. 'I'm so proud of you,' he said.

Sarra stood there in front of her child. Berenike wasn't sure what to make of her mother's actions, but one thing was clear: Sarra would have died for her daughter.

'I know where I get my stubbornness from now,' Berenike said with a grin.

Sarra stepped closer towards her and held her arms out to her daughter. As Berenike slowly embraced her mother, Michael witnessed for the first time the family he'd always imagined.

'There's somebody else who needs one of those,' said Sarra as she glanced over to Gabriel.

Berenike looked over at the Archangel. Today, he shone brightly in her eyes, the brightest she'd ever seen him. Gabriel waited patiently to embrace her. With the words Jovan uttered to her ringing in her head, Berenike began to look at him in a different light. It was hard for her to believe she could possibly love him more than she did, but today her love for Gabriel was as deep as it could ever be.

He reached out his hand to pull her close into his embrace. 'What is it? What did he say to you?' Gabriel remembered the look of shock on her face as he watched her defeat Jovan.

'I'll tell you later, OK?' she said. 'I love you.'

'And I love you, but if you ever do that again...' he said as he held her.

Uriel stood there, pacing anxiously. 'I have to agree with Gabriel. You scared us all,' he snapped at her.

Berenike could see how upset Uriel was; his emotions were visible for all to see. She embraced the tough and stern Archangel; Uriel wasn't used to so much affection, and it caught him off guard.

'You didn't see that coming, did you? Forgive me?' she asked Uriel as she squeezed him tighter.

Uriel couldn't help smiling. He was so relieved. 'Yes, I forgive you,' he said, smiling as she held him tight.

'Where's my hug?' asked Raphael.

Metatron rolled his eyes at him and shook his head. Uriel

laughed; Raphael could always make him smile.

Berenike hugged them all, then faced God. They all took their places beside her in front of their maker. She stood before him and went down on bended knee, just as Jovan had done, then looked up to find his arms were spread wide for her. She ran up the steps to hug God as he sat on his throne of gold.

'Thank you, child,' said God.

'Thank you for showing me the right way, and for being there with me,' Berenike said.

'Berenike, I've always been with you,' God said with a smile.

'Lord, what do we do now?' asked Michael.

'We clean up the mess. I have a feeling many things are about to change,' God said as he smiled at Berenike.

CHAPTER THIRTY-ONE

BETRAYAL

'Do they suspect anything?' asked Minion.

'No,' Gaige said as he sat on Jovan's throne. 'Don't worry. Jovan's time here is now over. He's where he belongs,' said Gaige. 'Gabriel will pay for taking her from me.'

Gaige had been making plans since he first saw Gabriel and Berenike together. His distaste for the Archangels had grown to an unhealthy level of hatred, and with all his memories back, he felt used. He felt she belonged to him and no one else. She was his possession, no other's.

His jealousy was beginning to consume him. Berenike was no longer in love with Gaige and hadn't been for quite some time; their Earthly relationship ended a long time ago with his infidelity. Although he'd protected her through several lives, his conduct showed him in an extremely different light. Self-gratification, lust, and a lack of consideration for others, all combined with disrespect.

Whatever he could gain for himself through each lifetime would be payment for keeping her safe.

'I want you to take a team to Heaven. Head to the seventh level and set each warrior in place. You will capture Gabriel and bring him to me.'

'And then what?'

'Then I will make him suffer.'

The hate for Gabriel he was exuding, filled Minion with joy as he clapped his hands together.

'You're my kind of leader, Gaige. I'm sure you'll enjoy keeping that throne warm.'

'I'm not keeping it warm, Minion. If Jovan does not want it, then I will be keeping it. Jovan is human now, so it will be difficult to guide him back to us. Anyway, I have plans for the underworld.' Minion's excitement was overflowing. 'It's time to catch a bird, my friend.'

Gaige was full of anger and hatred, and his deceit would play out in an act even God himself wouldn't see coming. The bond Berenike now shared with Gabriel was unbreakable.

Berenike was spending a lot of time with Gabriel now. They stood side by side as she watched Michael welcome new souls into Heaven. The new arrivals were from Earth and had lost the battle defending their home from Jovan and his army. Gabriel enjoyed watching her as she became more curious at what her father was doing, inviting each soul into the grounds of its new home.

'Gabe, what's he doing?' she whispered.

'He's blessing them and welcoming them into Heaven.'

She was troubled. 'Has God blessed me?' she asked,

swallowing hard as her throat tensed up. The thought of her not being blessed on a holy level had occupied her thoughts for quite some time.

Gabriel smiled lovingly and gently placed his arms around her. 'Dear one, you were blessed on the day you were born, on the day he sent you away, and every day after that - and you're a blessing to me.'

'Gabriel, you're my heart and my soul.'

He loved her; there was no doubt about it. He held her in his arms as tight as he could. Berenike giggled as her happiness overflowed.

'Not so icky after all, then,' said Michael. They both laughed as he joined them. 'Yes, you are a blessing. I couldn't be prouder of who you are.' Berenike smiled as her father's words filled her heart. 'Gabriel, why don't you both take the night off? There are enough of us here to guard the Heavens tonight. I'll see you in the morning,' Michael said, smiling as he winked at his daughter.

'Thank you,' Berenike whispered.

'Goodnight,' said Michael as he watched Gabriel and Berenike run off together like teenagers. His daughter was happy, and his best friend was filled with joy. Michael couldn't ask for anything more as a parent than for his daughter to be happy, and she was.

CHAPTER THIRTY-TWO

A LOVE LOST

As the sun went down, signaling the end of the day, Heaven was once again at peace. It hadn't been this quiet in a very long time. Michael had given Berenike and Gabriel the night off to spend some time together, the Archangels were content, and God was happy. Berenike had certainly earned it. The Archangels would keep guard on the Seventh Heaven for tonight.

As they soaked in the moonlight, they lay in each other's arms. The scent of flowers traveled throughout the Heavens. The aroma drifted into the horizon as they lay amongst the flowers, watching the stars. Their bodies were once again entwined, and the passion between the two of them secured the bond they had for one another.

'Are you going to move in with me?' Gabriel asked, kissing her neck. He took a deep breath and smelt her skin. Every single touch was as if they'd discovered each other for the first time. He couldn't get enough of her. She could feel the heat from his breath on her body, and she loved every minute of it.

'Gabriel, that's awfully human of you.' She was surprised at his question. 'Hmmm...it's a little sudden, but...' She giggled, teasing him.

'But?!' He laughed.

'Let me think about it,' she said as she kissed him.

'Have you thought about it long enough?' As his lips traveled across to the other side of her neck, Berenike's breathing became heavier.

'Will there… be…some of this… if I move in?' she said slowly to him.

'I promise there will be plenty of this.' He was almost as giddy as she was.

'I moved my pillow to your bed about an hour ago.'

'Really?' he asked, suspicious. He raised an eyebrow at her comment, then they giggled like children.

'Do you honestly think I'm going to spend any more time away from you?'

Gabriel took her into his arms. Within seconds, they were floating high up in the sky, ultimately reaching a height that would let them overlook the entirety of Heaven. As Berenike looked down upon Heaven, her heart was full of love for the beings of Eternity.

'Look at our home, Gabe. We saved it.'

Berenike was now looking at Heaven with different eyes. She could see the beauty in it she hadn't seen before and would be just as protective of Heaven as she was of Earth. He was incredibly proud of her and the fact that she not only saved Jovan, but that she'd also managed not to let Heaven fall.

As they made the descent back to the palace, they laughed and chatted as Uriel waited for them. He'd had been observing the two of them for quite some time now.

He greeted them with a smile. 'Hi, kids.'

'Hello, Uriel,' Berenike said.

Uriel couldn't help grinning. 'I'm sorry to do this to you. I know it's your night together, but Michael's called a meeting. Gabriel, you're required in the Holy Court.'

'I'll be there shortly,' Gabriel said.

As Uriel turned to leave, he noticed Berenike was a little out of sorts. 'You have grass in your hair, Berenike. Pleasant dreams.' He smiled as he left.

Gabriel plucked the stalks of grass from her hair, laughing.

'That Uriel is one cheeky Angel,' Berenike said with a giggle, then they both laughed.

'Why don't you head off to bed? The meeting won't take long, and I'll be back as quick as I can,' Gabriel said, missing her already.

'Gabe, when you get back, there's something I want to talk to you about,' Berenike said, nervous.

'Of course. Is everything all right, dear one?' he said to her as he kissed her goodbye.

She nodded yes. 'Everything is perfect.' *Everything will be fine,* she thought.

Gabriel stood in the doorway and took one last look at her before he left. He loved to see her smile and still knew how to make her blush simply with one look.

'Berenike, I love you.'

'And I love you, Gabriel.'

They were so incredibly happy together, Gabriel found it difficult to leave her. His place was firmly beside her now.

As Gabriel set out for the seventh level of Heaven, his mind was on Berenike. He smiled, thinking of her. Just the thought of her brought him an incredible amount of joy.

He walked from room to room, smiling. The closer he got to the throne room, he could feel a presence watching him. An uneasy feeling swept over him as he drew his sword. Gaige had sent several of what used to be Jovan's henchmen to Heaven. Lurking in the darkness was pure evil, with only one task: to capture Gabriel and take him to Hell. Gaige would make him suffer for taking Berenike away from him.

Before Gabriel knew it, several of them had set upon him and forced him to the ground. Their numbers were too many; he couldn't fight all of them. They gagged him and placed a hood over his head so he couldn't see. Although he couldn't speak, he still had his connection with the other Archangels.

As the Archangels all stood in the Holy Court, awaiting his arrival, Uriel could see what was happening.

'Brothers, Gabriel is in trouble!' he exclaimed.

As quickly as he spoke, they all raced to protect him, arriving right in the middle of an ambush. They all fought as hard as they could to save their friend. The Holy Grounds of Heaven were breached, and once again evil had been permitted to enter.

As Berenike lay sleeping, the Archangels fought hard to protect him but couldn't stop the henchmen from capturing Gabriel. The Archangels pursued them relentlessly to the far ends of the universe and back, returning just as dawn was breaking in Heaven.

'Who's going to tell Berenike? It will break her heart, Michael,' said Uriel.

'Don't you think I know that?!' Michael shouted. He was distressed enough without the reminder.

Try as they might, the Archangels couldn't find Gabriel anywhere, nor could they sense him.

Berenike awoke to find that Gabriel hadn't returned to her last night. She'd fallen asleep waiting for him and had slept through the night. Curiosity got the better of her, and she headed out to find him; her intuition was telling her something was terribly wrong.

As Berenike made her way out towards the balcony, the Archangels all arrived at once before her, minus Gabriel. Her alarm bells went off immediately; she knew something was wrong. She looked at them one by one.

'Father, what's going on?' she asked Michael. 'Where's Gabriel? He didn't come home after the meeting last night.'

'He didn't make it to the meeting last night, Berenike,' Michael responded.

Berenike was getting desperate, and she looked to her father for answers.

'We don't know where he is,' Michael continued. 'There was an attack here last night, and he was taken.'

Berenike's eyes widened as the panic grew inside her.

'We believe it was Gaige,' said Metatron.

'Gaige? What? I don't understand.' Berenike was confused.

'Gabriel was taken. We believe Gaige did it because you rejected him,' said Metatron.

'What? I don't understand. What Gaige and I shared was so long ago. It's in the past.'

'Obviously, he thinks otherwise,' said Metatron. He was worried for his friend. They all were.

'Uriel was able to pick up on that at least, so we do know it was his doing,' Metatron continued.

Berenike closed her eyes and tried to locate Gabriel. 'I can't feel him. Can anyone else?' she asked. 'Tell me!' she yelled as the tears welled in her eyes. 'Where is he?!' she yelled at Michael, who held his daughter as she

screamed. She continued to scream as the tears flowed from her, then fell to her knees.

Uriel closed his eyes at the sound of her screaming; he could feel her pain as it stabbed at his heart.

'I promise you, we will do everything we can to find him. Night and day, no matter what it takes,' Michael said as he held Berenike tight.

The other Archangels left Michael to comfort his daughter. They were feeling defenceless from the attack. Michael rocked his daughter like a small child, knowing she wouldn't smile again until Gabriel's return.

CHAPTER THIRTY-THREE

GABRIEL'S PAIN

As Gabriel arrived in Hell, Gaige wanted to make sure he knew who his captor was. The henchmen brought him into the throne room and instructed him to remain silent. Gaige had set up a shield surrounding Hell so no other being could enter or leave the grounds. This made it quite difficult to find Gabriel.

Gabriel remained blindfolded as they shoved him to the ground. As they removed his blindfold, he realised he was back in Hell. Standing in front of an empty throne in the darkness, his anxiety level began to rise.

'Gabriel, you've been brought here to answer for your crimes,' Gaige said, appearing before him and sitting on the throne. Gabriel was shocked; Gaige had become commander in chief of darkness.

'What crimes?' asked Gabriel.

'Your seduction and brain washing of Berenike! Take him away!' yelled Gaige.

'You're insane,' said Gabriel as Gaige's henchmen dragged him to the dungeons with his hands tied.

Gaige had his henchmen beat and lash Gabriel to the point where he nearly lost consciousness. He couldn't fight back; there were too many of them. After they tortured Gabriel until he could barely stand, Gaige appeared before him.

'Your mistake was obtaining her love for yourself,' he taunted Gabriel. 'You changed her. You Archangels believe you can have anyone you want, do anything you want. You don't own the heavens! I think it's time you learnt who is in charge.'

Gaige drew his sword as two of his henchmen forced Gabriel to his knees. They extended his wings and held them in place, fully extended. His hands were bound together. As Gaige moved closer to him and stared deep into his eyes, Gabriel could see the anger and jealousy within him. Gaige raised his sword above his head, lowered his blade, and cut repeatedly into Gabriel's wings, hacking at them until they were shredded into pieces.

As the feathers from what was left of his wings fell to the ground, Gabriel was defeated. The pain was excruciating as he screamed. He was beaten, and that was exactly what Gaige wanted. The bloody stumps that appeared through the skin on his back had several feathers still hanging from them, the blood dripping to the floor.

'Not so beautiful now, are you?' Gaige spat.

Gaige dragged Gabriel to a wall, chained him by the hands and feet, then left the dungeon. All Gabriel could do was wonder why. The attack was brutal. Gaige would be accountable to the Archangels when they found him, but Berenike's anger for what he'd just done to Gabriel would be unfathomable.

'Berenike!' he cried, his heart aching to be with her.

Several weeks later, Uriel went to visit Berenike. Still upset from the attack, they both sat in silence on the balcony. He cared for her a great deal, as did the others.

'Can you sense him yet?' Berenike asked, her voice hoarse from crying.

'No. He has not gone, Berenike. God would know straight away if he was. At least that's something to hold on to.' Berenike looked so incredibly sad. Uriel could feel her pain.

'This is my fault, Uriel,' she said.

Uriel didn't know what to say to her. She was inconsolable.

Berenike touched her stomach. The child growing inside of her was more important than ever to her now because if anything happened to Gabriel, the baby would be the only reminder of him they'd all have left.

'I want to talk to you about something, and I don't want you to get upset,' Uriel said.

'OK.'

'I know you're pregnant.'

Berenike was horrified he knew, and she suddenly grew scared.

'I saw Jovan's vision. Don't worry; I'll protect you until Gabriel's return.'

'Uriel, what happens when I start to show?' she asked. 'I'll have to tell Father.'

'Your child was made from love, Berenike; I can assure you he won't be angry.' She listened as Uriel spoke. 'We thought your birth was unprecedented, a human and an Archangel - but two Archangels? This is definitely a first. You do realise you've become more Archangel recently? It's far more dominant in you now. You're less human every day.' Uriel smiled at Berenike, trying to offer some form of comfort. 'I think Heaven will rejoice at the birth of your child. The heavens and all who reside in them will sing.' Uriel's eyes clouded white as he received a vision. 'Your father is going to be shocked, but he will warm to the idea. In fact, I think he will love being a grandfather,' he said as he smiled.

'Gabriel's absence is going to test you, but you know you have us all by your side, and of course you have me as well. You are not alone Berenike,' Uriel said to her in a gentle tone.

Berenike hugged him. If only Uriel could make everything better, she would stay in his embrace, but she knew she had to ride out the storm and pray for the return of her love. Gaige, on the other hand, was something she wasn't going to compromise on. His actions weren't something Berenike would easily forgive.

'Berenike, Gabriel loves you very much. You are the very air he breathes, and if I know him as well as I believe I do, you will not be far from his thoughts. Your love will get him through whatever he is enduring,' Uriel said.

'When you find Gabriel, leave Gaige to me,' Berenike said coldly.

Uriel nodded.

The Archangels spent every day regrouping to discuss their search plans for Gabriel. One day as they were discussing a possible location, Uriel collapsed with pain and cried out.

'Uriel, what is it?' asked Michael.

'Can't you feel it? It's Gabriel. What has he done to him? He is in terrible pain. We need to find him soon, or I fear he may not survive.' Uriel knew from the pain he felt that Gabriel was suffering badly. 'Do not tell Berenike. She's already broken,' he said.

CHAPTER THIRTY-FOUR

SHIELD AND SWORD

No sooner had the heavens opened, they closed once again. As the clock turned hour by hour into a new day, the veil that shielded humanity from the different planes of existence once again separated to protect the spirits that dwelled there. For those with a knowledge of what was beyond the veil, they now held close to their hearts that there was more out there in the universe. The events that took place during the battle for control of the Heavens had taken its toll on humanity. During Jovan's invasion, they unified as a race to protect one another. They also protected the Angels.

God would never forget the loss and sacrifice it took to regain and secure the Heavens. Humanity had witnessed and been caught in the middle of the battle for Heaven, and the Archangels were determined never to let it happen again.

The Seven Heavens would now have a new set of Guardians, new protectors for each realm and level. The one thing they'd all learned from the experience was that it wasn't enough to be a beacon of God's light delivering his message. The Guardians of Heaven all had to be able to defend each realm so they wouldn't be defenceless again.

They all had a purpose and would no longer be lapse in their duties. They would become warriors of the highest order. They'd believed nothing could ever topple the Kingdom above, but having come close to rewriting pure existence, they realised nothing is impossible; Berenike was living proof of that.

God had bestowed upon Berenike the very special honour of being his Warrior and guardian of the Seventh Heaven, his protector and chief warrior. She would now stand side by side with her father in protection of the spirits that dwelled there. The Seventh Heaven was the doorway before God himself. The final place before judgment. It was a true honour, and Michael was very proud of his daughter.

'Berenike, I have something for you,' Michael said, anxious. Berenike stood like an excited child waiting for her father's gift. 'Hold out your hands in front of you,' he said.

Michael then placed a large sword in her hands. The blade was long and thin right down to the tip, with an indentation formed in the middle of the sword that went right down to the bottom. She could see it was sharp as the point on the end began to glisten in the light. At the base of the grip was the symbol of infinity that looped around to form and symbolise strength and eternal bond of the warriors of Heaven. On the handle grip itself was a row of diamonds.

'Father, it's beautiful. Thank you.'

'I made it for you myself. I wanted you to have something from me, plus I wanted something to pass down to you. It's made from

Illyrian steel. Illyria was the city both your mother and her ancestors was born in, so it's quite ancient.'

As Berenike inspected her sword, Michael handed her a shield. It was round, and the designs on the front of it were very old looking and shined with the light of Heaven.

'Oh my, it's amazing, Father. What does the writing say?'

Michael smiled at her. He could see how excited she was at receiving his gifts. 'It says Child of God's light, daughter of Michael, and protector of the Heavens.'

Berenike kissed her father's cheek. 'Thank you, Father. It's perfect.'

The Archangels were all so very proud of her accomplishments. As Uriel stood amongst the crowd, he observed her looking over her shield. He smiled, as he was very proud of her as well. His fascination with her would now take on a life of its own.

His eyes shaded white as he received a vision: He saw Gabriel in the dungeons of Hell. As he delved closer into his vision, he watched Gabriel suffer through torture after torture until finally succumbing to his fate. Uriel looked further to see Berenike in his arms and the two of them enjoying the life she and Gabriel had always hoped for. He was stunned. His feelings for her were developing, but not at the cost of his friend's life, he thought as he tried to shake the vision.

Berenike saw Uriel amongst the other angels, and she ran to him and hugged him tight. He embraced her, then touched her cheek as his heart gave in to his affection for her. Berenike was thrilled to see Uriel was there to share her special moment with God and father. The only one missing was Gabriel.

'Uriel, I saw you just had a vision. Was it of Gabe?' she asked.

'No, Berenike.' Uriel felt guilty for lying to her but couldn't bring himself to lose what little moments he could share with her.

He quickly changed the subject so he could talk to her. 'Your shield is magnificent. Your father outdid himself on this one,' he said, smiling as he inspected Michael's work. 'He loves you very much, Berenike.'

Berenike nodded yes, smiling.

CHAPTER THIRTY-FIVE

THE REALISATION OF MANY THINGS

From day to day, Berenike would look down at the Earth and view what she used to know as everyday life and its people. She kept a constant eye on Jovan, who'd been banished to Earth, reduced to the level of mere mortal, filled with all the memories of his now past life. Jovan was now living in Berenike's house. She'd put him to work in her store, and with Amy and EJ's assistance, he was learning to be a human being.

'Tell me, child, what do you see?' said God.

Berenike took a deep breath and looked down on the Earth to observe. 'They've changed,' she said. 'Humanity...it's like their eyes have been opened. There's no longer any doubt...well, for most anyway. I see love in their hearts, and I see a genuine change in them. It's like they've all been in a state of sleep and now they've awakened.'

'Then why are you so troubled?' he said.

Berenike's eyes widened. She was surprised he could see through her efforts to hide her emotions.

'It bothers me how easy it is to get in here. Jovan nearly destroyed you. If he could do that then, it'll be easy for anyone to break into Heaven as well. And now with Gabriel missing...' Her voice cracked. 'I never knew hate and jealousy could be that powerful,' she said. 'It's funny; before I arrived here, I used to think Angels were just beings that existed in story books. I had no idea how complex you all are and how similar you are to human beings.'

'Tell me,' God said, curious.

'You have the same vulnerability, compassion, stubbornness and will that humans do. You feel the same emotions, and you deny them as well. Your Angels really aren't that different from human beings, you know.'

God laughed at her comment. 'I forget sometimes how bright you are, Berenike.'

As Berenike observed her surroundings, she thought about her transition into Heaven. 'Everything here in Heaven is bigger, better, more serious and far more beautiful than anything I've ever known. Everything is larger than life. You feel everything more. Emotions seem to be heightened here as well.'

God smiled at her. 'Berenike, that's because this is where everything begins. This is where I started creation. By the time you reach your earthly body, you're only half the being you began as,' he said to her. Both Berenike and God looked out of the palace window, down on the Earth, to see Jovan. 'We must always be on guard with him. Keep that in the back of your mind. Never be complacent, and never forget the sacrifice that's been made to protect this Kingdom,' he said to her.

'I promise you, I will always serve the Heavens and protect what it represents,' Berenike said as she looked God in the eye. Her honesty made him smile. She then watched Jovan and felt a sense of sadness as tears came to her eyes. 'What he's going through isn't really that different from what I went through when I arrived here. I had help, but he doesn't; not really,' she said sadly. 'Amy and EJ will do their best

for me, but I know deep down Amy would rather Jovan wasn't there. He tried to destroy our planet...well, nearly.'

'Don't let your compassion for him cloud your judgment. Your forgiveness of Jovan is more than I expected. You are the being I have always hoped he would be. Just be careful not to walk his path. You must remember, there are rules, and they must not be broken,' God said.

'Did he love my mother?'

'No, child, he envied her and your father. He wanted what Michael had with her, but I think he knew he would never find it, and that's why there was so much conflict within him,' God said, looking at Berenike's reaction. 'His jealousy turned to hate, and his hate to evil.'

'That's one messed up Angel.'

'I only have myself to blame, child.'

'Oh, I wouldn't be too hard on myself if I were you,' Berenike said. 'Angel or human, you gave us free will, and the choices we make are what shape us. We know right from wrong,' Berenike said to him.

'He gave in to evil. His lust for power and vengeance took over who he was, and as an Angel, there is no room for both,' said God. 'He had the world, but he let his behaviour get the better of him. I'll never understand why.'

'You know, I had a taste of how evil felt. His seduction was tempting,' Berenike said as he looked at her, concerned. 'It was like eating chocolate. Too much can make you sick!' She giggled to herself.

'What stopped you?' God asked. He was curious.

Berenike thought about his question and smiled. 'Gabriel,' she said.

God paced the room behind her. 'Berenike, Jovan was my most loved of them all. My most magnificent being. I modeled all my Angels off him. A perfect creation, which eventually took on a life of his own. I did not count on humanity getting in the way.' The events of the previous weeks had bothered him a great deal. 'Jovan's fate is still yet to be decided,' he said.

'Well, if it's OK with you, I'll keep an eye on him,' Berenike said.

God nodded in agreement.

As Berenike closed her eyes, God could feel the pain she'd been shielding from him whilst trying to keep her secret. She ached for Gabriel, and the worry inside her was consuming. Her heart was broken. She was suffering from the loss of her love and betrayal from someone she cared for. She wanted revenge against Gaige for his crime, and she would have it once her love was safe.

God smiled to himself as he realised she was carrying Gabriel's child within her. 'Child, Gabriel will come home safely. We will find him; I promise you,' he said to her.

'I love him, and I know I'm breaking the rules with our duty to Heaven, but...'

God didn't let her finish her sentence as he said, 'I know you do, child, and I can see he loves you. I have seen it for quite a while now. We all have.' He took Berenike's hand, and they sat down together on the steps that led to God's throne. He was very fatherly. 'I made a mistake with your parents many years ago. I should never have sent you away, dear girl. I hope you can forgive me, but I did it to protect you. Maybe you and I can make a fresh start?' he asked, smiling at her.

'I'd like that,' Berenike said to him, smiling.

'Berenike, when Gabriel returns, I will allow it,' he said. 'Your child will need its father, as well as its mother.'

Berenike looked at God, stunned. She kept forgetting he was an all-knowing God.

'Thank you,' she said as she hugged him. She wasn't sure what to say to him, but at that point it didn't matter.

'You know, Berenike, Gabriel is one of my children. I miss him too,' God said.

It had never occurred to Berenike that God would be feeling the loss of one of his own creations. Gabriel is a Prince of the Heavens and a child of God. She hadn't given much thought to the fact that God was a parent as well.

'Why can't you see him, Lord?' Berenike asked, confused.

'Something very powerful is shielding my sight. Wherever he has taken him, he does not want me to find him. Your father is out there every day, looking for him, Berenike. He won't stop until he brings him home,' God said as she wiped the tears from her eyes. 'What have you learnt so far?' he said to her.

'The love and light of God will always win over evil,' she said to him, smiling. 'It has to.'

'Go and see your father. He's missed you long enough.'

As God smiled at Berenike, he knew Heaven would never be the same again. She was a beacon of light that had changed them all, and she would now be fierce in her protection of Heaven.

CHAPTER THIRTY-SIX

A CHILD WITHIN

Berenike headed to the balcony outside the archives. She could see the Archangels, including her father, all standing there in conversation as she entered the balcony. Fearlessly, Berenike approached Michael. There was no better time than now to tell him about the baby. She looked to Uriel for approval, and he smiled and nodded to her; his approval made it easier for her to face her father.

'You have to find Gabriel, Father,' she said.

'Berenike, we will. I promise you. We are all out looking for him, and we will not stop. You know that,' Michael said to reassure his daughter.

As he continued his conversation, Berenike tried again. 'Please bring him home to me.' She then took his hand and placed it over her stomach.

Michael's expression changed to a look of complete shock. 'Berenike...' he said.

Raphael and Metatron didn't take long to grasp what was going on, and Uriel signaled for his fellow Archangels to leave so Michael could be with his daughter. As they all left the balcony, Michael took Berenike's hand in his.

'Does Gabriel know?'

'No. I'd planned to tell him the night Gaige took him. Jovan told me just before I stripped his powers.'

Michael observed his daughter's tear-stained face and smiled. 'My little girl.'

Berenike snuggled in closer to her father's chest, feeling safe in his embrace.

'Father, I can't have this baby without him,' she said.

'I will find him. He will be home soon. I promise you,' Michael said as Berenike held on tight to her father. He felt it was his duty as her father to bring Gabriel home to her and his grandchild.

'I want you to let me deal with Gaige when you find them,' Berenike said.

'What do you mean, Berenike?' Michael could sense a coldness to her words. Each day Gabriel was away from her, her light diminished just a little bit more.

Her sadness was darkening her heart.

'Berenike, revenge is not the way. It's not God's way.' Michael was concerned. 'You must leave his punishment to God.'

'I'm so scared for him, Father. Just the thought of what Gaige might be doing to him...'

Michael held her tight. 'I am too.'

The Archangels stood back, watching them. They were worried for Berenike, more so now that she was carrying Gabriel's child.

'Well, that was unexpected,' said Raphael.

'Was it really?' said Uriel.

'None of us could have imagined that, Uriel, but we owe it to them both - and to the baby - to bring him home.'

'She wants revenge, you know. We'll have to keep an eye on her,' said Uriel.

'What about what Jovan said to Michael? The Prophecy?' asked Raphael.

'It may not be her the prophecy is about, and anyway, it's up to us to make sure that never happens,' said Uriel.

'It's time to find Gabriel,' said Metatron.

As the Archangels continued to search for Gabriel, Berenike stood on the balcony, looking deep into the light. She was wearing the gold dress Gabriel had given to her as a gift; it made her feel closer to him even though he wasn't physically there. She closed her eyes as she ran her hand across her stomach, then thought of a name for the baby and smiled. She would now wait for Gabriel's return.

God found himself walking through the Heavenly Palace, taking in his surrounding. He was still concerned with the fact that they hadn't yet found Gabriel. Six months had passed, and each day God could see Berenike's light withering away inside her soul.

As God made his way slowly back to the throne room, he traveled up the stairs of the great staircase. When he reached the throne room, with a wave of his hand He removed the barrier that separated the veil between his throne and the seventh level of Heaven. He sat down on his throne and glanced over at the empty throne that sat next to his own. God had sent his Son, Yeshua, on a search to find Gabriel. If anyone could find him, it would be his son.

"My son, what have you found?" he asked.

"I have found Gabriel, Father."

God stood up from his throne, anxious to hear his son's words. 'Where is he?'

Yeshua appeared before God in the throne room. God hugged his son, then Yeshua sat down next to his father.

'Father, Gabriel is in Hell. He's in quite a bad way, and we need to get to him soon. I was able to see him, but it will take a strong force to break down the barrier shielding us from him.'

God was distressed at what he'd just heard. "I think we both know what force that will be. What else?" he asked his son.

'Gaige has taken the throne of Hell. There is a great darkness surrounding him, Father. He also has someone helping him. It's Minion.'

'All right, I will call my Archangels. They need to be informed of this.'

God knew Michael would be anxious once he heard they'd found Gabriel. Nothing was more important to him than bringing Gabriel home to Berenike.

CHAPTER THIRTY-SEVEN

NEW LOVE

As the days passed, Berenike's pregnancy progressed rapidly; time in Heaven passed quite differently than on Earth. Berenike had now found many natural remedies in Heaven to help her relax and ease the stress of Gabriel's absence, and as she wandered barefoot through the grounds of Heaven, she found a swimming hole in a remote section of Heaven. She removed her clothing and immersed herself in the warm waters of Heaven, her body relaxing as the warmth of the water covered her skin.

Berenike leant up against the edge of the pool, rested her head, and closed her eyes. Within the silence, she could hear the ripples of the water as they began to flood her skin. As Gabriel's body pressed against hers, she felt the sensual touch of lips on her neck. His touch made her heart race as he pressed his naked body against hers.

Suddenly jolting awake, Berenike caught her breath, opened her eyes, and felt the ache in her heart start all over again.

'No,' she cried.

She stepped out of the pool. As she reached for a towel to dry herself, she saw Uriel standing before her. His hand touched hers, sending a tingle though her body as he passed her the towel. Berenike dressed as he watched her; he couldn't take his eyes off her as her skin disappeared within her clothing. She could feel the upset rising within her, and she began to cry. Uriel held her in his arms, and as she pushed her face into his chest, he squeezed his eyes shut and enjoyed her embrace.

'Berenike, what's wrong?' he asked, his voice soft and gentle. He kissed her forehead, then her cheek. Finally, he gave in to his feelings for her and kissed her. As he moved her body in closer to his, the fire within him ignited.

Berenike pushed him away. 'Uriel, I'm so sorry. I really didn't mean to do that,' she said.

Uriel bowed his head in shame. 'Berenike, it's my fault. I apologise. Forgive me,' he said, then bowed, left her side, and flew into the sky.

Berenike sat on the edge of the rock pool, thinking about her actions. She knew she was missing Gabriel, but she didn't realise Uriel had feelings for her.

In the distance, a spirit was approaching her. The soul was unfamiliar. She stood up to greet it.

'Hello, Berenike. I see you've found a place to hide,' she said. 'My name is Amatiel. I look after this side of Heaven when Yeshua isn't around. I'm sort of like the caretaker here." She raised her eyebrow and smirked. 'Yes, I'm the caretaker of the pond.' They both giggled.

Amatiel was stunning. She had dark hair with pale skin. She was very tall and quite slender. She stood quietly as she looked over

Berenike. She was a being without wings, obviously from a different part of the galaxy to Heaven.

'How are you enjoying Heaven?' asked Amatiel.

News of Berenike's arrival in Heaven had reached the far end of the universe. There were some who were still in fear of the prophecy coming to pass, especially now that Berenike had a child on the way.

'It's beautiful here, and it's nice to be back in my father's life. It's not what I expected at all. I just wish…'

'You wish Gabriel was here. We all do. He is greatly missed, but it won't be long before he is home now that Yeshua has found him.'

Berenike was startled. 'He found him? When? Why wasn't I told?'

'Berenike, he's only just arrived back. Didn't Uriel tell you? I know he came looking for you.' Amatiel was surprised Uriel had kept such important information from her.

"No. He didn't. He was here with me, but I don't think that's what he had on his mind."

Amatiel looked confused.

Berenike was furious no one had told her, and even more angry at Uriel. She flew up into the sky to reach the Heavenly Palace, then stormed up the great staircase and into the throne room.

CHAPTER THIRTY-EIGHT

YESHUA

God had summoned his Angels to appear before him, and soon Michael, Uriel, Metatron, and Raphael all appeared in front of God, along with Ariel and Haniel; they'd all been out looking for Gabriel and Gaige. As Michael arrived, he could see Yeshua had returned.

'Lord, you're home! Welcome back!' said Michael.

Yeshua stood up from his throne and hugged Michael. 'I see you have much to tell me, Michael. I see your daughter has come home.' Yeshua was looking forward to meeting Berenike, but he was concerned about the distress she was feeling with Gabriel's disappearance.

'My Archangels, my son has found Gabriel,' said God.

They were all relieved. All but one. All but Uriel.

Uriel's demeanour changed at the announcement of Gabriel being found. Yeshua could feel the change in him immediately.

'Michael, you will need to plan a rescue. It won't be easy to access Hell. Gaige has taken the throne and created a barrier blocking access in or out. It's why we haven't been able to see in.'

'Gaige has taken the throne!?' exclaimed Michael.

'Michael, let Berenike know my son has found him. She will be pleased,' said God, smiling.

'I will tell her!' said Uriel.

Michael frowned at how eager Uriel was to see her. He was now watching her very closely, and Michael was concerned Uriel was developing feelings for her while Gabriel was away. Michael knew how much his daughter loved Gabriel and hoped she would set Uriel straight.

'Michael, I'm looking forward to meeting Berenike,' said Yeshua.

Michael smiled. 'I think meeting you will be good for her, Lord. It will get her mind off things for a while.'

Yeshua smiled. 'I see a lot has changed here since I have been away looking for Gabriel. What is going on with Uriel? He seems very protective of Berenike,' he said as he watched Uriel leave.

'Yes, it's like he's her bodyguard now. None of us can get anywhere near her.' Michael frowned, and Yeshua could see the look of concern on his face. 'Don't worry. I'm keeping an eye on it, my Lord,' said Michael.

Suddenly, Berenike appeared and ran as fast as she could into the throne room. 'Father, is it true? Where's Gabriel?' she asked, anxious to hear the news of Gabriel.

'He's been taken prisoner in Hell, and he's badly hurt. Gaige has taken the throne. He's had him there since he was taken. He's also shielded us from his sight; that's why God can't see him,' said Michael. 'Yeshua has been looking for him as well. Haniel and Ariel went with him, and now they have found him.'

Berenike looked over to observe two archangels she'd never

met. They bowed their heads to her as she smiled. Berenike then leaned around her father to see behind him. As her eyes widened, she caught a glimpse of Yeshua, only to find him staring back at her, amused. Berenike was nervous; she was about to meet God's son for the first time.

'Berenike, I want you to meet Yeshua,' said Michael, guiding his daughter towards Yeshua.

Yeshua stood up, stepped down from his throne, and walked closer toward them both. As he stood in front of Berenike, he stopped and smiled. He was very gentle looking as he reached out his arms to her, and he certainly didn't

dress the way she expected; there were no robes, just a long white shirt and white trousers with long sleeves, very simple in style. Understated yet crisply white, with simple shoes that looked like they dated back to his time on Earth. To her, he was quite the bohemian when it came to his clothing attire. Meanwhile, his hair was as mainstream religion had written, dark brown and just over his shoulders in length, with a very soft, flowing look about it as it fell around his face. His eyes were blue, with a gentle sparkle about them. The first thing that popped into her head was that they were full of life, and his face radiated pure love, just as it did with God.

'Hello, Berenike. It's so nice to meet you,' he said.

Berenike struggled to get the words out. 'Hello,' she said as quietly as she could. 'You're not wearing robes?'

Yeshua laughed. 'No, I like to keep them for more official duties,' he said, winking at her.

Berenike just stood there, speechless, not knowing what to say. Finally, she took a deep breath and said, 'Father said you found Gabriel.'

'Yes, Berenike. Why don't we talk? Let's take a walk in the

gardens. I hear you have done some work to brighten them up,' said Yeshua.

Michael watched them both leave. He was relieved Yeshua was home and Berenike might be able to calm her thoughts. They walked towards the gardens, past the Ascended Masters graveyard, where they sat on a seat Berenike had prepared. As they sat on the park bench, she could see Uriel in the distance speaking with the locals. She could feel her blood start to boil; her anger was rising.

'He loves you, Berenike,' said Yeshua. 'He didn't mean to, but he does.' She didn't expect Yeshua to be so blunt.

'Well, I love Gabriel,' she snapped back.

'We all know that, but just keep in mind Uriel is hurting too. He's confused about how he feels about you and his loyalty to Gabriel. He loves you both, and he's struggling with it.'

'You found Gabriel. I don't understand. We've all been looking for him for six months, and no one has been able to find him. How is it you could?'

Yeshua took Berenike's hand in his. 'Berenike, I am the son of our creator,' he said, raising his eyebrow at her.

Berenike looked him over. He was larger than life to her and quite the enigma. At that point, she realised he was making a joke.

'Can I ask you something, my Lord?' she said. Yeshua nodded. She turned to face him so she could look him in the eye, then turned his hand over to look at his scar from the crucifixion. 'How is it you can forgive humanity for what they did to you?' she asked.

Yeshua smiled at her intrigue. 'My love for you all is bigger than any wrong you could ever do. Berenike, humanity has the greatest potential I have ever seen. There are some souls that stray off their path that is written in their soul contracts to enter the Earthly plane, but there are also souls like you who show so much good in them, and such greatness, you can't help but believe in the goodness of humanity. Souls like you are what inspire me to forgive. When I see someone like you, I can't help believing in them.' Berenike smiled. 'You have the ability to forgive. You just need to remember that,' said Yeshua. 'The forgiveness you showed Jovan is the same forgiveness you must have for Gaige.'

Berenike was annoyed at his comment. The thought of having to forgive Gaige for hurting Gabriel...she knew she would have to dig deep within to find that forgiveness.

'But it's not the same, Lord. It's just not,' she said. Yeshua frowned. 'So, tell me about your Kingdom,' she asked.

'Don't change the subject, Berenike!' said Yeshua. He was being quite stern with her. 'You must forgive Gaige for what he has done. Like I said, some souls lose their way.

'Do you want Gabriel to forgive Gaige for what he's doing to him as well?' she asked.

'Berenike, when Gabriel comes home, you will need to be there for him to help him heal. His path to recovery is intertwined with yours. I'm concerned if you don't forgive him, this anger will consume you and darken your heart. I don't want that for you. You shine the brightest light in our Kingdom. I haven't seen that since Jovan. If I must step in, child, I will, but I would prefer you discovered the forgiveness within, by yourself.'

'You were betrayed by a friend, someone you loved. Did you forgive him? Did you forgive Judas for what he did?

'Berenike!'

Yeshua was surprised at her. She was making valid statements, but she was coming from a place of hurt, not a place of love, as he'd hoped she would. Her human side was showing, and it was stronger than ever before.

'Berenike.' He sighed heavily. 'Yes, child, I did forgive him. I loved him as a brother. Judas was aware of the part he was required to play in my journey. He didn't want to, and he didn't like it, but it was written long before he was chosen to be part of the story. My death paved the way for what you all now call Christianity. Without my disciples spreading my Father's word, we wouldn't have so many souls here in Heaven…would we?' Her large blue eyes held his stare. 'The journey is about love and forgiveness. Does that answer your question, Berenike?'

She took a deep breath as she whispered to herself, 'Forgiveness. Hmm…I'll have to work on that one.'

'I see my Father has bestowed upon you guardianship of the Seventh Heaven. It's a great honour. You must be an example to other souls.'

'Yes, it is, and I'll protect it and those within these walls,' she told him.

Yeshua smiled. 'I have no doubt about that. My Father has chosen well.

Berenike watched as Yeshua began to tense up like Uriel did when he received a vision.

'You just had a vision, didn't you? I didn't realise you had those.'

'Your world wasn't ready for me, Berenike. Maybe soon, now that many souls are waking up and remembering who they are, but yes, I used to have them all the time on Earth.'

'Beautiful and perceptive. You must really keep Gabriel on his toes!'

Yeshua laughed. 'Your greatest test is yet to come, Berenike. You have some time yet, but it will take place after your child is born.' Berenike felt scared, but she still had Gabriel to worry about. He would remain her focus for the moment. 'Would you like to know who it is you're carrying?' he asked. Berenike nodded yes. 'You have a son, dear girl,' he said.

'I have a boy...?' she said as tears of joy flowed from within her. She embraced Yeshua and held on tight. Besides finding Gabriel, it was the best news she could have received.

'Let's talk again, Berenike.' She nodded, and he reached over to squeeze her hand. 'I promise you, child, you will smile again.'

Yeshua stood up to leave and smiled. Berenike realised she'd finally met the most famous being there ever was, and he was real. As he disappeared into the light of Heaven, she perused her surroundings and saw Uriel approaching in the distance. She stood, angry and fierce, awaiting his arrival.

CHAPTER THIRTY-NINE

REVELATION

Berenike's blood was on the boil as Uriel approached.

'Hello, Berenike. I've been looking everywhere for you. There's something I have to tell you,' he said.

'Bet your ass, there is!' Berenike snapped.

Uriel was quite startled by her comment. She pushed at his chest over and over, attempting to pick a fight with him. She punched Uriel in the face, and the intensity of the blow had him reeling across the field where he stood only moments earlier. Like an enraged street thug, Berenike would make Uriel pay for not telling her the news of Gabriel. She chased after him, and while he was still on the ground, she kicked him.

Raphael observed the melee from the throne room, looking out across the heavens. 'Michael, I think you'd better see this. Your daughter is out of control,' he said. Michael looked out the window to see what Raphael was talking about. 'I think you should stop her. You know she's probably the only other person who can hurt him besides God. She seems very angry, Michael,' Raphael said.

'By the looks of things, I think it might actually take the two of us to break this up. Come, Raphael, help me deal with my daughter,' said Michael.

As Berenike raised her hand to punch Uriel again, he stopped her, taking her into his arms and flying her into the sky as high as he could go. She screamed uncontrollably in response.

'Berenike!' Uriel screamed. 'Stop this!'

He knew he did the wrong thing but didn't realise how much it had hurt her. Berenike kept screaming at him, yelling and punching him. Finally, Uriel could think of only one thing that would stop her: he kissed her. She had no choice but to give in, and she weakened in his arms.

'Uriel, stop, we can't do this,' Berenike said, but the more he touched her, the more she wanted him. Her body wanted to give in to him, but her heart was screaming to be with Gabriel.

Uriel flew higher and took her to a secluded area of Heaven. She was still in his arms as they landed. 'Berenike, I love you. I can't help it, and I can't fight it anymore,' he said. He kissed her again, and as she weakened, she finally kissed him back.

'We can't do this. It's not fair to Gabriel,' she said.

She allowed him to kiss her over and over as she initially gave in to him, but then she pushed him away. 'Uriel, I'm sorry, but I can't. We can't be anything but friends. I love Gabriel. I'm carrying his child, Uriel - did you forget?!' she said to him in a gentle tone.

'No, Berenike, I can't forget,' he snapped back at her.

Berenike then plucked up the courage to ask, even though she was scared of his answer, 'How long have you known where he was?'

'A while,' said Uriel. He couldn't look her in the eye; he was too ashamed. Berenike was almost sick. 'I can be a father to your child, Berenike, please let me. I will love him like he is my own. I will love him as much as I love you. You care for me too, I know you do.'

Berenike was so shocked at what she was hearing from Uriel, she had to sit down. 'Uriel, of course I care for you,' she said. 'But I love Gabriel. I don't want to be with anyone else but him.' She could see the tears welling in his eyes. 'I'm sorry I hit you.' Though she apologised to him for her actions, she couldn't look at Uriel, as she was ashamed of him. Instead, she flew off into the Heavens, but Uriel followed her like a puppy.

As they arrived back at the palace, they were greeted by Raphael and Michael. Berenike could see the concern on Raphael's face as he approached her. He saw her as his little girl as well, and the sight of her anger had distressed him that she was capable of such actions. Michael could see the bruises that had formed on Uriel's face from the fight; he'd taken quite a beating from his daughter.

'Raphael, please take my daughter to the throne room. I'll be there soon,' Michael said. Raphael nodded. 'What is going on with the two of you?' asked Michael. Uriel just stood there and said nothing. 'Uriel, I know you have feelings for her. I understand that, but you're confusing her.'

Uriel was still distressed. 'I love her, Michael,' he said with a sigh. 'Don't worry, though. She made it clear it's Gabriel she wants,' he finished, wiping the blood from his cheek.

Michael raised his hand to his face to heal him. As his light shone, both Uriel's bruises and wounds disappeared within it.

'Uriel, Berenike's extremely vulnerable right now. Maybe you need to distance yourself from her for a while,' Michael suggested. Uriel's eyes widened with distress at the thought of not being able to be near her. 'I've seen how you both look at each other.' Uriel couldn't deny it. 'You look at her the same way Gabriel does.' As Michael spoke, he could see how hurt and frustrated Uriel was with the situation. 'She will never be yours, Uriel. She loves Gabriel too much. Every time you touch her, she will always be thinking of Gabriel. I am sorry, my friend,' said Michael.

Uriel was hurt by Michael's words, however true they may be.

Michael returned to the throne room to deal with his daughter.

CHAPTER FORTY

BERENIKE'S REMORSE

Berenike returned to the throne room with Raphael and awaited her father's reprimand. She knew she was wrong for attacking Uriel, but she didn't expect him to say he loved her.

'Are you all right, child?' asked Raphael.

Berenike didn't want to talk about Uriel's feelings for her, as it would expose her own behaviour.'Uriel knew about Gabriel and didn't tell me,' she said.

Raphael was shocked as he thought about what she said. 'Maybe he wanted to be sure first before he said anything to you?'

'No, Raph. He had all the information he needed. He didn't tell me because he didn't want to.' Berenike looked out of the window, resting her head on the edge of the window pane. 'When is he coming home to me, Raph? I don't want my son to grow up without his father; it's too cruel. Forever longing for a parent who doesn't exist. You know I'm six months pregnant and haven't felt the baby kick yet?'

'Child, we now know where he is. Your father and I will bring him home to you, you know, that right?'

Berenike nodded yes. Raphael didn't quite know what to say to her. They all missed Gabriel, but Berenike's heartache for the loss of Gabriel had turned into physical pain.

'Are you sure Uriel knew?'

'Yes, Raph. Why haven't we gone after him yet?'

'I think your father wants to discuss a rescue plan now that we know where he is,' he said. 'With the barriers up that Gaige has created, I think we may need you to break them down, but we can talk about that soon.'

'Soon! We should be going now!'

She kept staring ahead out into the horizon of Heaven. Michael had arrived earlier and heard the conversation between the two of them. He knew Berenike was struggling with the loss of Gabriel, but he didn't realise it was affecting her pregnancy. Yeshua was right to be concerned over her.

Raphael kissed her on the forehead and left the room as Michael approached his daughter. Berenike could feel her father standing behind her as he placed his arms around his daughter to hug her. She smiled to herself; she'd missed having a father over the years.

'I'm sorry about my behaviour earlier, Father. Yeshua had just finished telling me I need to be an example. What a great example I've been.'

'I'm sure he will understand,' said Michael.

'Berenike, why didn't you tell me how you were feeling?' asked Michael. As Berenike shrugged her shoulders, Michael looked into his daughter's eyes. All he could see was pain.

'Is Uriel badly hurt, Father? I feel terrible.'

'I think you both need to talk, but probably give him some time. He's nursing his ego right now,' Michael said with a smirk.

'I was so angry at him. He's known all this time, Father.' Berenike could hear Michael sigh as she cried. 'I thought he cared about me?'

'Berenike, he does care about you; that, I'm sure of. I think he had other intentions for not telling you. Either way, I'm sure God will deal with his behaviour later.' Michael held her as he listened to her cry. 'I've asked your mother to come spend some time with you. Would you like that? You can have some mother and daughter time together,' Michael said to her as he smiled.

'OK, that would be nice. Thank you, Father.'

CHAPTER FORTY-ONE

NATHANIEL

Gabriel sat in the dirt of his holding cell, his face and body stained with his own blood. He watched the guards take one prisoner after another to be tortured, and the sounds of the prisoners screaming began to frighten Gabriel, spiking his anxiety level. Gaige would make his hatred felt throughout the dungeons of hell.

His cell mate, Nathaniel, was as curious as Gabriel as to whom would be taken next. There wasn't much more either of them could endure, as their bodies were being brutally tortured. Gabriel had noticed very few who were taken survived their ordeal.

Gaige accompanied the guards to collect Gabriel from his cell. 'Hello, old friend,' he spat, then ordered his henchmen to take Gabriel to the lower depths of Hell, where his hands were chained to a post and he was whipped from head to toe.

It had been several weeks since Gabriel had seen Gaige, and he noticed Gaige was looking quite different. His face was older, his skin pale. He'd been in the darkness for many months. Stress lines had appeared on his forehead, and his eyes had a deep coldness within them. He'd aged, purely from the hate he felt towards Gabriel and the Archangels.

'Look at me!' Gaige yelled. As he grasped Gabriel's hair between his fingers and pulled his head back to look into his eyes, he could see the angel within him. 'You're still in there, I see. Well, not for long.'

He raised his hand to punch Gabriel, then repeatedly struck him over and over. Gabriel was defenceless. With his hands tied to the post, all he could do was take punch after punch from him. The assault was brutal, more than any human could ever endure. Gabriel imagined looking into Berenike's eyes for comfort. Whenever he was taken to be tortured, he would think of the one thing that gave him comfort, and that was Berenike.

The guards took Gabriel back to his cell and threw him to the ground. Nathaniel did his best to comfort Gabriel by bringing him water and guiding him to rest. His body ached from head to toe. Both Gabriel and Nathaniel had reached their limits, but Gabriel's torture was far worse than Nathaniel's. Neither of them was strong enough to fight back. All Gabriel could do was have faith in the fact that he knew Berenike wouldn't give up trying to find him.

'You're awake,' Nathaniel said, wiping the blood from Gabriel's face. 'I don't know how you are surviving this, Gabriel. She must be very important if Gaige is making you suffer like this.'

'She is worth dying for,' said Gabriel.

Nathaniel smiled and said, 'Tell me about your Berenike.'

Gabriel sat on the ground of his cell as he thought deeply of his love for her. 'She is not only the protector of eternity, she was born with the light of God within her, although she is full of fire,' he said, smiling. 'She is love and light combined, and she is all you imagine good to be. Within her heart is the light we all seek to find.

She is the daughter of an Archangel. She is more than just my twin flame, she is the very air I breathe, and I will see her again.' Gabriel sighed. 'I miss her.'

His declaration brought a tear to Nathaniel's eyes. 'Well, if you feel that strongly about her, I can only imagine how she feels about you,' he said, smiling. 'You know who I am, don't you, Gabriel?' asked Nathaniel.

'Yes, brother, I know you are one of the fallen. I sensed it when I arrived here. In fact, I sensed quite a few of the Archangels,' said Gabriel. 'How long have you been here?'

'Since Jovan's first attempt to take the Heavens. This is where we came after our Father locked us out of Heaven.' He smiled. 'Yes, a very long time, although it's only been since Gaige took over things that it's become more violent here. He had me locked in a cell when he found out I was an Archangel, along with some of the others. Many of us were tortured and placed in the dungeons. At least now I know why he hates us so much.'

'I am sorry, Nathaniel,' said Gabriel.

'Don't be, Gabriel. It's obvious he's off the rails. Maybe when your girl rescues you, she can rescue me too,' said Nathaniel.

Gabriel smiled as he leaned back against the wall and closed his eyes.

CHAPTER FORTY-TWO

THE LOVE OF A MOTHER

Berenike left the seventh level of Heaven and proceeded down the staircase that led to the top of the palace, God's place of residence. Her mind was occupied with thoughts of Gabriel; her heart missed him. She stopped on the sixth level and sat on the steps by herself as she tried to connect telepathically with Gabriel. Her vision took her through several dark rooms, leading to a chamber where she saw Nathaniel and Gabriel. She gasped.

'Gabriel, can you hear me?' Gabriel's chin had lowered to rest against his chest, and he jumped as he heard Berenike's voice. 'Gabriel, if you can hear me, my love, I'm coming for you. Please stay strong.'

Gabriel was alert and listening. 'Dear one!' he said, smiling. 'I can hear you,' he said as the connection was lost. It didn't matter. Gabriel had heard her voice, and he knew she was on her way to him.

Berenike sat there, thinking about Gabriel coming home to her and her son. She rubbed her stomach and said, 'Your daddy will be home soon.' The child she was carrying was more important than ever.

Berenike sat there quietly as she observed a light coming out of the darkness. As it came closer toward her, she felt an overwhelming feeling of warmth in her heart; her mother had come, just as Michael said she would.

'Mother!' Berenike screamed out loud as she flung herself into Sarra's arms like a little girl. Berenike was thrilled her mother had come to see her.

'Your father said you needed me. I've been waiting for you to call for me, but you haven't,' Sarra stated quietly.

'I'm sorry, Mother. I've just had other things on my mind.'

'Berenike, please let me help you get through this,' said Sarra.

Berenike smiled at her mother's declaration. 'I'm OK, Mother. I don't need to get through it; I just need Gabriel home. Anyway, did you hear they found Gabriel?'

Sarra frowned. All she wanted to do was help her daughter, but Berenike wasn't letting her in.

'Sweetheart, you're not alone. I'm here for you.'

'I know, Mother. I'm OK.'

Sarra knew she had to break down walls with her daughter but didn't realise they were rock solid. 'Berenike, you told Raphael the baby hasn't moved yet?'

'Everything will be OK, Mother, I promise. Gabriel is coming home soon, and everything will be back to normal.'

'Alright.' Sarra's mothering instinct was front and centre. 'Berenike, I didn't get to be a mother to you for very long, but I would love it if you would allow me to be that to you now.'

Berenike held her mother's hand. 'Well, I could do with some help in the nursery,' she said.

Sarra smiled with relief. 'You may want to hold off on that for a while. I think Yeshua has something in mind for the baby to sleep in.'

'Really?!' Berenike was excited.

Sarra was thrilled to finally see some joy in her daughter's face. Earth history had claimed Yeshua's profession as a carpenter, so to have the son of god create a baby's cot for her and Gabriel was something very special.

'He wants to give you a special gift for the baby.'

'I thought that would be something Father would want to do?' Berenike said curiously.

'Berenike, your father makes swords, not cots.'

They both laughed. The thought of such a military man building a cot for a baby was humorous to the both of them.

'Yeah, I see your point,' Berenike said with a laugh.

She and Sarra sat together as they talked about the past. Berenike had many questions to ask her mother.

'Mother, what was it like for you being a mother?'

'Your father and I were thrilled when I became pregnant with you. We couldn't have been happier, but then there was Jovan. His jealousy destroyed him. Your father and I were happy together, but of course it was forbidden. You know that, don't you?' Berenike nodded. 'I always knew you would be special.' Sarra smiled at her daughter. 'Berenike, I loved you and will always love you. I will always be your mother no matter how much time separates us.'

'Oh, Mother.' Berenike embraced Sarra. To hear those words was all Berenike needed to move forward. 'Maybe we could spend the day together?'

Sara agreed. 'Of course we can.'

CHAPTER FORTY-THREE

JOVAN'S HUMANITY

It was some time before Amy and EJ reopened Berenike's shop. After the destruction caused by Jovan in the battle, they, like everyone else, either had to rebuild or renovate from the damage. As Berenike requested, Jovan was put to work in the florist, with Amy and EJ overseeing his life to adjust to being human.

As Berenike watched Jovan from the Heavens, God watched her as she shook her head over and over.

'What's wrong, Berenike?' he said.

'My Lord, it's Jovan. He just abused one of my clients,' she said with a heavy sigh.

As God watched on, he could see Jovan's behaviour not only scared the staff, it also scared the customers away.

'Linda's the only one standing up to him. I need to go down there and give him a reminder as to why he's there. I'll have talk to Amy as well, I think. She can't let him do that.'

Jovan had no sooner finished arguing with Linda than he headed to the back of the shop, where he laughed and sniggered at his own antics. Berenike quietly arrived at the shop and stayed invisible as she watched Jovan tidying and sweeping dirt out the back door as he muttered to himself under his breath. He could sense a presence with him. Although he wasn't an Archangel or the King of Hell, he could still sense the angels when they were around him.

'I know you're there. You may as well show yourself,' he said. Berenike appeared as she walked out of the light before him. 'Wow, you're so fat now,' he exclaimed.

Berenike took the paperwork from the counter and hit Jovan across the head with it. 'I'm pregnant, you fool!'

'What do you think you're doing?' he yelled as she hit him over and over with the paperwork. 'Berenike, stop hitting me.'

'Never say that to a woman. You're lucky it's the paperwork!' she said. 'Stop being rude to the customers. Have you forgotten I can see what you're doing?' Her finger pointed north. 'You can't speak to people like that.' Jovan remained quiet as she scolded him. 'Look, I know you're having trouble adjusting to being human, but you have people who want to help you, so let them - and if you don't mind, I'd appreciate it if you don't run my business into the ground.'

Jovan laughed. 'Actually, its Amy's business now, so I guess I'm running her business into the ground,' he said proudly. He laughed uncontrollably, then regained his composure.

'Berenike, why did you send me here? You did this to punish me, didn't you? Are they all laughing at me up there?'

Berenike was shocked at his declaration. 'Jovan, you would have been destroyed if I hadn't. Plus, I wanted you to see what life is like as a human being.'

'Well, I hate it!' he yelled. 'I'm powerless here.'

'Yes, you're supposed to be.' She raised an eyebrow at him. 'You're the least of our worries up there, by the way.'

She had his attention. 'What do you mean? Trouble in paradise? Not the happy couple anymore?'

'Gaige kidnapped Gabriel and has taken him to hell.'

Jovan was genuinely concerned. 'Gaige has the throne, and no one stopped him?! What is wrong with you all?' Jovan seemed genuinely upset. 'At least I was strategic and had a plan when I was in charge, but he's just plain full of hate. He's just a soldier. He's not even an Archangel.' Jovan was now stating the seriousness of the situation. 'In many ways, Berenike, he's more dangerous than I was.'

Berenike started to cry before him. As she broke down, Jovan didn't know what to do as he watched her crumble before his eyes.

'How long has he been gone?' he asked.

'About 6 months. We only just found out he's in Hell. Uriel knew and didn't tell me, and now everyone is just standing around doing nothing when we should be trying to rescue him.' Jovan was concerned as he listened to her distress. 'Jovan, I saw Gabriel in Hell. I don't think he has much time left. We need to rescue him, and soon. He's not in a good way at all. I need him home in my arms.'

Jovan could see Gabriel's absence had darkened her light and removed her smile, one of the things he found captivating about her. 'Berenike, your light's fading,' he said. 'I don't have much of a purpose here. There isn't a lot to fulfil me except fighting with Linda - and she's quite feisty, you know,' he said, smiling. 'There is something I can do that would make me feel part of it all again if you'll let me.' He had Berenike's attention as she wiped the tears that had now become regular to her face. 'Let me help you plan an attack to rescue Gabriel. Who better than me to help you find your way around inside the walls of Hell? Tell the others to come to me tonight, and I can speak with your father.'

'And in return, what is it you want?' Berenike was curious.

'Nothing. Consider it my debt fulfilled.'

'Alright. I'll see if Father will come,' she said as she disappeared into the light.

Jovan returned home and sat in the same chair Berenike had fallen against just before she passed into the heavenly realm. He thought about his life in hell and was curious as to what Gaige was up to. As he sat in the darkness of Berenike's lounge, he enjoyed the comforts of humanity by drinking his whiskey and ice as he awaited the arrival of his old counterparts. He was lonely. As he remembered his life back in Heaven, he remembered his love, Lilith, who was part of a very distant memory that would forever stay buried deep within his heart. As his mind wandered, Jovan remembered how they held each other's hands as they walked through the Garden of Eden. He thought about her smile and the feeling of her lips on his.

'So long ago, Lilith,' he said, smiling.

Within the darkness, Jovan could see the light of several beings coming toward him; they revealed themselves to him as Michael, Raphael, Metatron and Yeshua. As they all stood before him, instinct took over and he was down on bended knee in front of Yeshua.

'There is no need for that, Jovan. We are here to listen to what you have to say,' said Yeshua.

Jovan stood up and guided them to sit at the table, then proceeded to draw a map of Hell.

'Berenike had a telepathic link to Gabriel at one point. She saw him in the dungeons, chained to a wall,' said Michael.

'The dungeons?! Well, you also need to know there's a torture chamber close to the prisoners' cells.'

'You designed this, Jovan?'

'It served its purpose, Michael. Why haven't you been able to access Hell? There's an open door policy, you know. I never rejected anyone who wanted to come to me, so why can't you get in now?'

'You know yourself how powerful hate is. Gaige has built a new empire based on his hatred of Gabriel and the Archangels,' Michael responded.

Jovan thought about what Michael just said, then asked, 'You could just let me come with you, I could show you the way around?'

'No, Jovan, we need you to stay here just in case anything happens,' said Yeshua.

'Well, I did feel the full force of your daughter, Michael, so I don't think you will have any trouble getting in there.'

They both grinned, then as they discussed the easiest way to infiltrate the walls into Hell, Jovan and Michael slowly built an understanding that they needed to work together. This time around, there would be no power struggle between the two of them.

Jovan held out his hand to Michael. 'Good luck, Michael.' Michael nodded. 'I'll be here if you need me,' said Jovan.

'I know,' Michael said with a nod, then smiled at Jovan as he disappeared into the light.

CHAPTER FORTY-FOUR

MIND GAMES

'Minion, have they finished torturing Gabriel for the day?' Gaige asked.

'Yes, Sire, they have returned him to his cell,' said Minion. 'Sire, I don't think he can take much more. Do you have any further plans for him?'

'No, Minion, I think it's time we ended his existence. I'm sick of the sight of him. Mark him for execution!' Gaige exclaimed.

Minion jumped up and down, clapping his hands.

'I'll do it myself,' Gaige stated.

'May I watch, Sire?'

'You may, yes, Minion.'

Gaige headed to Gabriel's cell to let him know his time was just about up. He would gloat and seethe as the competition for Berenike's affection was about to be ended in such a way that would change things forever.

Berenike was now tired of waiting for her father to save Gabriel. Now was the time to unleash hell on Gaige, and if she could, she would make him pay for hurting the man she loved. A part of her humanity she wasn't letting go of was her anger.

As usual, Uriel was in the ancient archives, reading up on Earth history. He took great interest in the happenings of Earth and why human behaviour was like it was due to free will. Berenike flew into the archives and headed straight toward Uriel. She'd startled him, but he regained his composure and smiled.

'Hello, Berenike,' he spoke softly to her.

'Uriel, I'm sorry I hit you,' she said, but his lovesick grin made her feel like slapping him again. 'I need your help.'

'Anything. Whatever it is, yes. I will do anything for you,' said Uriel.

Berenike noticed how desperate his words were. 'Firstly, stop that. Secondly,' she hesitated, 'I want you to come with me and rescue Gabriel.'

Uriel knew he had to make things right with Berenike. 'Alright. What do you have in mind?'

"We go there, now, and we storm the cells. I'm strong enough to break the force field down, but I need you as my back-up just in case anything goes wrong.'

Uriel nodded in agreement, then said, 'We should wait for your father, Berenike.'

'No, I'm done with waiting.' Her response was short and abrupt. She wanted Gabriel back in her arms and would do whatever it took to achieve her goal.

Uriel and Berenike headed to the armoury. She took the sword and shield her father gave her for battle, and Uriel took his blade, a magnificent sword that shone with the light of the heavens, capable of blinding a human eye purely with its shine. Although quite different from Berenike's, the handle formed a cross design at the handle grip, which was gold, whilst the rest of the blade itself was thin and silver. It suited Uriel perfectly, as it was two different sides of the spectrum, being both gold and silver. Uriel and Berenike flew into the sky, then proceeded through the dimensional wall into the depths of Hell. Surprisingly, there was no need to use her light to break the entrance down; the veil was already down and completely unguarded.

Berenike stepped into the darkness of the dungeons, with Uriel close behind her. They searched from cell to cell until they reached the very end of the main corridor. As Berenike walked into the remote section of the chamber, she saw Gabriel. Uriel grasped her arm to pull her back toward him, and they hid and observed Gaige as both he and Minion prepared for what looked like an execution.

'Hello, Gabriel. This will be the last time you see me. In fact, this will be the last time you see anyone. The time has come for you to pay for what you've done,' Gaige said.

Minion and Gaige both removed the weakened Gabriel from his chains and dragged him to the platform for execution, where he was chained again, and this time his hands were tied behind his back. Gaige raised his sword to diminish the light from Gabriel once and for all, but before he could lower his blade to Gabriel's neck, Berenike appeared from the darkness with Uriel and let off a blast of light of her own, throwing both Minion and Gaige across the room.

She had Gabriel's attention as she yelled, 'Hang on, Gabe! I'll only be a moment - I'm just taking out the trash!' Berenike was a woman scorned, and with her hormones racing from the pregnancy, her anger was quick to reach a very dangerous level of aggression.

'Dear one!' Gabriel gasped. He was physically in a bad way, but that couldn't wipe the smile off his face. 'Brother!' he yelled as he saw Uriel attack Gaige.

Minion crept up behind Uriel and knocked him to the ground, where he lay motionless, out cold. Gabriel tried to gather the strength to help Berenike against Gaige, but he was too weak to fight.

'You shouldn't have come here, Berenike,' said Gaige.

As Berenike spun her sword around her wrist like a pro swordswoman, she circled the enemy - and Gaige caught a glimpse of what was under Berenike's cape, and he wasn't happy.

'My God, you're pregnant. Is it his?' Gaige asked as he pointed to Gabriel.

'Yes, this is the child of the man I love.' Berenike was smiling as she signaled Gabriel.

Gaige caught her off guard as he used the back of his hand to strike her across the face, then she fell to the ground.

CHAPTER FORTY-FIVE

RESTORATION

Berenike and Gaige wrestled on the ground in front of Gabriel, who had very little strength to help as he screamed, 'No!'

Gaige pinned Berenike to the floor of the cell. As he held her down, he ripped at her clothing and tore open her shirt to find a large baby bump, Gabriel's child. Gaige was so irate, he punched her in the face as she screamed.

'How dare you carry this parasite within you?! His child?!'

Gaige was beyond reason at that point, and he raised his sword above him to strike at Berenike's child.

Uriel was awakened by the commotion of battle. As he came to, he quickly got up off the dungeon floor and thrust his sword into Gaige, who dropped his sword as Berenike saw a blade come through his chest. As he fell, she managed to wriggle out from under him. She saw Uriel standing there behind Gaige; he'd ended his life in protection of the woman he loved. As she got up and ran to Gabriel, Uriel broke the chains with his sword and released him from his prison.

Berenike didn't let Gabriel go. She kissed his face over and over as she welcomed the light back into her heart. They both cried as they embraced each other. Gabriel was very weak, as the energy had virtually been drained from his body.

'Time to go, brother' said Uriel. 'Get him out of here, Berenike. I'll be with you soon; I'm just going to tidy up a bit,' he said with a grin.

'Uriel, Nathaniel is still here,' Gabriel said. 'They took him away earlier. Gaige has taken revenge on the Archangels here. You must find him. It's time for him to return home as well.'

Uriel nodded at Gabriel's request. 'I'll find him and get him home. You must go now, Gabriel.'

'Be careful,' Berenike said as she hugged him. 'Thank you, Uriel.'

Uriel kissed her. He knew it was the last time he'd be able to do that. Unfortunately, Gabriel had just witnessed Uriel's love for her; he'd seen the kiss.

Berenike was exhausted. She'd managed to get Gabriel to safety, but they weren't home yet. Uriel had sent them to a cave that was halfway between Earth and Heaven, and they were safe for now. As they entered the cave, Gabriel was losing consciousness, his light rapidly diminishing. Berenike lay him down on the dirt of the cave and looked over his body, which was bruised black and blue. He had cuts and blood from one end of his chest to the other, but the most shocking of all was his wings; they were in pieces.

As her heart filled with love, she placed her hands on Gabriel's body and closed her eyes. The light soon shone throughout the cave, lighting up his body as he transformed back to his Angelic form, complete with wings. He sat up and looked into Berenike's eyes as she fainted; the power within her needed to heal was more than she had at that point, with the pregnancy taking most of her energy.

Gabriel gently sat her up against the wall in the cave as she slept, deciding to stretch his legs a little whilst keeping her within his sight. He stood at the entrance to the cave as he felt the light of Heaven come through the entrance. He then closed his eyes, stretched out his wings, and let out a sigh. It felt good to have his wings back, and even better to have his love back in his arms.

Gabriel sat down in front of Berenike whilst she slept, watching her. After a few moments, he opened her jacket, which Gaige had ripped during his attempted attack on her, then placed his hand on her stomach as his eyes filled with tears. He was completely overcome with joy, and there was no better homecoming than that. Gabriel leaned in to kiss Berenike as she slept, and her eyes opened to see his beaming smile.

'It worked,' she said as she threw her arms around his neck, kissing his face over and over as she cried. He held her as her tears subsided. 'I'm so sorry, Gabriel, this is all my fault. He did this to you because of me. I'll never forgive myself for what he's done to you.'

'Berenike, please, don't do that. I don't blame you. It was his actions, not yours, dear one,' Gabriel said to her.

He examined every inch of her face. 'I thought of you every single day. It kept me going. How long have I been gone?' he asked.

'A little over six months,' Berenike said as the tears ran down her cheeks. 'I've missed you so much.' He ran his hand over her tummy. 'It's a boy. You have a son, Gabriel,' she said. 'I was going to tell you the night you were taken. Jovan told me before I changed him, and Uriel had a vision at the same time.'

Gabriel smiled as he nodded. He couldn't take his eyes off her. She was glowing for the first time since he was taken.

Uriel had arrived and was hiding, listening as he heard Berenike speak.

'I love you,' she said to Gabriel as they kissed.

It was in that moment Uriel knew Berenike would never love him the way he cared for her. Gabriel was her one true love, and that was all there was to it. Uriel loved them both. Now at least his affections for her would be put in the right perspective.

'I saw what he did to you. Your body was a mess,' Berenike said as she broke down. 'Your beautiful wings were all broken,' she said as she touched his cheek.

Gabriel's face saddened. 'Well, it looks like we can add healing to your list of skills now. That's my girl.'

'Yes, I am,' she said as she snuggled into him. They sat in each other's arms. 'Why did he do this to you, Gabe?' Berenike asked. She needed answers.

'Jealousy, hatred, spite, take your pick. He wanted you back. You were supposed to be his prize for a job well done. I don't think he expected us to fall in love.' They both smiled. 'The only explanation I was ever given was that you loved me and not him.'

'I'm so sorry, Gabe.'

'Hey, enough of that, OK? We have other things to worry about.'

'What do you mean?'

'Berenike, you're pregnant. I don't think this has ever happened before, definitely not between two Archangels, that's for sure.' Berenike was amused by his comment. 'I'm going to be a father.'

Berenike burst out laughing. It was the first time she'd laughed since he was taken. 'You'll be the perfect father, Gabriel,' she said. 'Let's go home.'

Gabriel whisked her up into his arms, then stretched out his wings as he took flight in the sky. As they flew through the heavens, Berenike snuggled into his chest as he held her in his arms. They flew into Heaven and over the main balcony of her favourite place. Still cheek to cheek, she remained in his arms as he paced the balcony, holding her. Gabriel sat down, placed his hand on her stomach, and felt the baby kick; Berenike was startled as she realised the baby had kicked for the first time. He lifted her blouse to see for himself, and beneath her bare skin was the child they'd made from the love they shared. They could see movement underneath her skin of either an arm or a leg pushing out.

'This is the first time he's kicked. I haven't been able to feel him until now,' she said, smiling. 'Gabriel, welcome home,' she said.

Michael finally found Berenike after realising both she and Uriel had gone missing. He'd suspected she'd gone after Gabriel.

'Yes, friend, welcome home,' said Michael, sitting down with them. 'Now that's a smile I haven't seen in a long time,' he said, smiling at his daughter. 'You should have waited for me to go with you.'

'Father, there was no time. When Uriel and I arrived in Hell, Gabriel was about to be executed. We got there just in time.' Michael nodded his approval. 'Has Uriel gotten back yet?' she said.

'Yes, and he brought an old friend with him as well, Nathaniel.' He directed the comment at Gabriel. 'Nathaniel said you shared a cell together.'

'Yes, Michael, we did,' Gabriel confirmed.

'I'm glad you're safe, both of you. I think I'll leave you two alone for a while. I'm glad you're home, Gabriel. We've missed you,' Michael said with a smile.

'Thank you, friend,' said Gabriel, smiling.

As Michael left, he glanced back at the two of them together and smiled. His daughter was happy again.

'So, have you thought of a name yet?' Gabriel asked her.

Berenike nodded. 'Yes, I was thinking Dominic. It means light of God,' she said with a smile.

'I like it.'

'So do I.'

Michael accompanied Gabriel to see God. They entered the throne room, and as Gabriel saw his creator, he ran to him and embraced him.

'Gabriel, my Prince, you are home. Thank goodness you're safe.' God held Gabriel tight, thankful he was safe. 'Are you alright?' he asked.

'I think so, Lord.'

'Will you allow me to heal you, Gabriel?'

'There is no need, my Lord. Berenike healed me.' Gabriel was smiling at that point, beaming with pride.

'She healed you?' Gabriel nodded yes. God was surprised but very happy. 'I have spoken with Nathaniel. He's told me what you went through.' He delved deeper into Gabriel's mind to see his thoughts. 'Gabriel, Berenike never gave up. I am yet to speak with her, however I can now see how much you both love each other. How much she loves you. Never doubt it. You are her twin soul. Know this, Gabriel, she would have died for you to save you.'

'But I saw him kiss her.'

'Gabriel, let me show you what happened between them. Let me show you the truth,' said Michael.

Michael and Gabriel stood before God as Michael projected a vision of Uriel and Berenike. He showed his daughter's rage, her tears, and of course her love for him.

'Gabriel, do you understand now? She never gave up on you. Just because Uriel developed feelings for her, doesn't mean they were reciprocated.'

Gabriel understood and was now able to see through the fear. He left the throne room and headed straight for Berenike, flying in over the balcony to their bedroom, where she awaited his return. As his feet landed on the floor, the vision of Berenike before him, next to God, was the most beautiful his eyes had ever seen. He took her into his arms and kissed her, her soft eyes making his heart and body yearn for her as they gave in to the passion they both shared for one another. The touch of his fingers on her skin relieved the ache that had resided in her heart during Gabriel's absence, and once again their hearts and souls burned as one.

With Gabriel now comfortably back within the fold, Berenike headed to Earth to see Jovan. She arrived in her lounge room to see him drinking again. He had a difficult day being human, and alcohol was now his crutch.

'Bad day, huh?' she said, materialising before him.

Jovan jumped as she startled him. 'Berenike!' he exclaimed, happy to see her.

She sat down on the lounge beside him. 'Hi, I just wanted to say thank you for your help in rescuing Gabriel.'

Jovan was confused. 'But I didn't do anything,' he said.

'But you did. You gave Father directions to the cells, but above all else you wanted to help, and for that I'm grateful. Gabriel's home now.'

'So, the rescue went well, then. How is he?'

'He's fine.'

'Well, going by how much you're glowing, I'd say he's more than fine.' Berenike giggled. 'It's nice to see you smile again,' he continued. 'You've got your shine back.'

His heartfelt comments made her blush. No sooner had they enjoyed the laughter between them, Berenike doubled over in pain.

'The baby's coming. It's too early for this.'

Jovan helped her to the bedroom, where she began the many stages of childbirth. 'Berenike, remember, Heaven works on linear time, not on Earth time. Your baby is coming, and I'd say it's not early at all. In fact, I'd say the time is right.' Her eyes widened in fear. 'I want you to stay calm and remember your birthing classes.'

'What?! I never took any!' Berenike screamed. Jovan was now the one who was scared. 'I need Gabriel here, and get Amy too.'

Berenike screamed for Gabriel to come to her side. As Gabriel appeared before them, Jovan directed him to sit with Berenike for support.

'Gabe, I need Amy here too. Will you please bring her here?'

'Yes, another woman here, that's a great idea! Hurry!' Jovan was nervous.

It was the first baby he'd brought into any world, although he'd always watched from the sidelines. It was now real; as real as it was going to get. Gabriel raised his hand and closed his eyes. Amy was at work when Gabriel projected her to join them, and since she was cutting hair, she quite conveniently had a pair of cutting scissors in her hand. When she appeared before them and realised what was happening, she sprung into action, assisting Jovan.

'Berenike, this is it, we need you to push.'

Berenike pushed as hard as she could as she screamed from the pain. Within seconds, the baby arrived, and the sight of the new little boy brought tears to Jovan's eyes; he was proud of helping bring her and Gabriel's son into the world. Amy took the baby, wrapped him in a white blanket, and handed him to Berenike. As Amy handed the boy to Berenike, she kissed her best friend's cheek.

'Congratulations, you two,' she said happily.

'Thank you, Amy,' said Gabriel as he reached for her hand. 'Boy, are you going to have a story for EJ tonight.' Amy laughed at the comment.

A few hours later, both Berenike and Gabriel were ready to return to the heavens with their son. Gabriel lifted them both into his arms as they prepared to leave.

'Thank you, Amy. I'll come back and see you soon, OK?' Berenike said.

'You better bring my godson with you,' said Amy.

'Of course, Aunty Amy.' The two best friends had just secured a stronger bond between them.

Gabriel stood before Jovan and took him into his embrace as he spoke. 'Thank you, brother. I won't forget what you did for us.'

Tears formed in Jovan's eyes at Gabriel's heartfelt declaration. He was overcome with emotion. Amy held his hand as the new family headed home to Heaven.

'I'll see you all soon. I love you both,' said Berenike as they left.

Gabriel and Berenike flew into the throne room with God and the Archangels all present. As Gabriel proudly presented Michael with his grandson, God blessed the little boy with truth, love, and when he came of age, the knowledge of the universe. Dominic's wings were now present and would grow to Archangel status, becoming as magnificent as his father's.

As the days passed, Berenike and Gabriel enjoyed the time spent with their new son. God also enjoyed spending time with Dominic. He would sit in God's arms as the Archangels had their meetings and discussed the growth of the universe and expansion of humanity. God was proud to take on the role of Great Grandpa, with Michael embracing the love of his grandson.

CHAPTER FORTY-SEVEN

WINGS OF AN ANGEL

Berenike paced the balcony with Dominic in her arms. Since arriving home at heaven after the birth of Dominic, Berenike's back had been constantly itching and tingling. The intensity was increasing as the hours passed, and it was now getting to the point where Berenike was finding whatever she could use to scratch her back for relief.

Michael and Raphael had joined her on the balcony to spend time with Dominic. Berenike loved the balcony, as it was the same place her father had stood with her to feel the rays of God's love the first time she arrived in Heaven. She stood quietly, enjoying the conversation with her father and Raphael. Yeshua and God decided to join them and see how Dominic was progressing. They were all chatting when Berenike had a surge of energy fill her body.

'What is it?' Michael asked his daughter. He could sense the energy flow close by.

Just as Berenike was about to answer him, she screamed. 'Quickly, take Dominic from me,' she cried.

Yeshua took Dominic into his arms as both Michael and Raphael rushed around her.

'What is it, child?' Raphael was worried. They all were.

As Berenike was overcome with pain, her body draped over the balcony as she screamed again. 'It's my back.'

The itching she'd been feeling since Dominic's birth had been becoming more and more intense each day. As they all tried to listen to what she was saying in-between the screaming, Raphael could see something under her clothing. He ripped open the back of her dress to expose what was underneath her skin, which bubbled and moved like it was about to erupt.

Berenike's scream was blood curdling. Raphael watched as two white wings unfolded from her back, looking on in wonder at what was happening to her. 'Child, don't be scared. You're getting your wings,' he said.

They were all quite shocked at what they were seeing before them. Berenike's screaming had gotten the attention of the other inhabitants of the Heavens, and the more painful it was for her, the softer the singing from the angelic beings before her. As they all rallied around her to soothe her screaming, Gabriel came running to her side. She gripped at the sleeve of his uniform.

'Raphael, what's happening to her?' he asked. His distress matched the excitement from Raphael on the balcony.

Tears were flooding Berenike's face as they rolled down her cheeks and rested on her chin. The pain she was feeling was like nothing she'd ever felt before, not even childbirth. They were all powerless to help her.

'Gabriel, she's becoming an Archangel,' said Raphael.

'Why are you doing this?' Michael asked God. He was terribly distressed at the sight of his daughter's pain.

'Michael, this isn't me. I've never seen this happen before. My Archangels were born with wings. You've seen that with Dominic.'

Raphael tried to calm Berenike down. 'Child, do you understand what is happening to you?' he asked, and she nodded yes.

All Raphael could do was sit and wait with her. Meanwhile, Gabriel took her into his arms to hold her. The pain would come in waves, as would more of the wings as they pushed their way out of her back. Michael stood close to his daughter to see for himself. Berenike's hair had turned white from shock. As she looked into her father's eyes, he looked back at an almost physically unrecognisable vision of his daughter. Her hair was now as white as the clouds, and her eyes were the colour of sapphires. She was now 100% pure Archangel, a true child of the light. As the last section of her wings was revealed, they could all hear the angelic sound of God's choir. The angels were rejoicing at the birth of another Archangel.

Berenike's wings were now completely out of her body, and she could now stop and regain her composure.

'Gabriel, how do I look?' she asked. She was nervous as she awaited his answer.

'Dear one,' he said as he completely looked at her from head to toe, then took her hand in his. 'Do you remember what I said to you when we walked across the Rainbow Bridge and into the gardens?'

'You said to me that I would be beautiful to you in any form.'

'Today, you shine the brightest I've ever seen. My love for you always has been and will be eternal. You are more beautiful today than I've ever seen you. Didn't you say you've always wanted wings?'

Berenike smiled as he kissed her. 'Raph, do you think anything else is going to happen to me?'

'I'm not sure. How do you feel inside, child?'

'Top heavy,' she said as they all laughed.

God took Dominic from Yeshua and brought him to Berenike. 'I think I might be able to help with that,' he said, then raised his hand to give her the balance she needed.

Berenike took Dominic into her arms. As he looked into his mother's eyes, his small hand reached out to her. She kissed his forehead. Gabriel was right: it didn't matter what form she was in; they would still know her.

Sarra and Metatron heard Berenike's screams and came rushing in to see the vision of their daughter and friend before them.

'Sarra, come.' Michael directed Sarra to stand with him and behold the new version of their daughter.

Sarra was hesitant. She held Michael's hand as she approached her daughter. Berenike smiled at her mother. She could see how scared she was for her.

'It's OK, Mother. It's me.'

'Berenike, you're magnificent.' Sarra touched her daughter's hair and inspected her face and eyes. 'There's my girl.' She could still see her daughter in there.

'So, how does it feel?' asked Metatron.

'It feels…OK.'

'With your transformation will come a new knowledge of the Universe.'

'I don't understand what you mean, Metatron.'

'Alright, let me explain it in terms you will understand. You're downloading like a computer does. All the wisdom of the Universe and all its secrets, you will now understand. Everything you have ever wondered about, all the questions you have asked will now be answered, as they are within you. Today is your Heavenly Birthday, Berenike. Happy Birthday, Child.' Metatron was absolutely thrilled at the transformation.

Berenike stood beside Gabriel, holding their child, and for the first time since her arrival in Heaven, even though she'd been home for a while, she finally felt like she belonged.

EPILOGUE

ARCHIVE OF MEMORIES

Berenike walked through the halls to the archives of the Heavenly Palace. Each night, she would put her son Dominic to bed, then make her way to the history records Uriel had shown her years before. She made herself comfortable as she sat down in the large wooden armchair Gabriel had made for her so she could nurse Dominic. She spent many a night documenting the events of the past since joining her father and the Archangels in the Kingdom of God.

As Berenike opened the book of records, she smiled to herself. The memories came flooding back like a river. She remembered when she first joined Michael in Heaven and how frightening it all was, realising she was destined for many things to come. She said goodbye to her Earthly life, along with her friends and the life she knew before, only to embrace the most magnificent existence she was now a part of.

Berenike had begun a new life as a being of light. She was now completely Archangel. Although the years in Heaven had forced her angelic side to the surface, it was now obvious where her ancestry laid. It was now more dominant than even she was willing to admit. So much had happened to her in the years that passed since leaving her Earthly body.

As she sat there thinking of the past, she could feel a familiar presence breathing on her neck. Gabriel's kiss greeted her with a welcome hello.

'I knew I'd find you here.'

Berenike looked into the eyes of the love of her life. What she felt for Gabriel was beyond any Earthly love. They were a part of each other now.

'What are you writing about?' Gabriel was curious. He knew she was spending a lot of time in the archives but wasn't exactly sure why.

Her hand gently touched his cheek. 'I'm recording my memories of the past. I think it's important for those who come after us to know what happened.' She struggled verbalising the words.

'What happened?' he quizzed her as he raised an eyebrow. She couldn't lie to Gabriel; he could see through it even if it was meant with the best of intentions.

'OK, just in case it happens again,' she said.

'What is it?' he asked. Gabriel could always tell when something was bothering her, as she was always so full of light.

'When I read back on what we've all been through, I honestly can't believe we're all still here. So much has happened, Gabe.' He took her hand and led her over to the lounge, where they could sit together and talk. 'Your arrival here certainly changed many things, but I wouldn't have it any other way.'

He kissed her cheek as she blushed. Through the silence, they could hear the small footsteps of a child coming toward them both.

'Mama, I can't sleep. Can I sit up here with you and Daddy?'

Before they could answer, Dominic climbed up on the lounge in-between his parents. They both looked at each other as their hearts softened at Dominic's request. It was a rare occasion when their son would be awake at night, so they gave in to his request.

'Alright, but only for a little, while then back to bed, my little Cherub,' she said.

Dominic was so excited to be awake with his parents. As the three of them cuddled, Michael joined them.

'Grandpa!' Dominic yelled.

'Hey, Champ,' Michael said as he hugged his grandson. 'I see you're not in bed.' Berenike's parental frown was directed back to her father.

'Mama, will you tell me a story about the Archangels?' Dominic asked Berenike.

'Well, OK, but then you have to go to bed,' she said.

Dominic shook his head yes. As Berenike began to tell the story of Heaven and the Archangels, the others joined them in the archives.

'Wow, everyone's here, Mama,' Dominic said as he looked around the room at the beings before him.

'Not everyone, my darling,' she said as she kissed him.

Jovan was missing from the group, as was Uriel. As Berenike's eyes met his, Michael knew exactly who she was referring to. Her sadness at not being able to unite them all as a family showed, but for now all would remain as God had commanded. The book on Jovan's fate was still not yet finished, and Uriel was nowhere to be found since Berenike and Gabriel had returned with Dominic.

'OK, so I'm going to tell you a story of the most magnificent beings in existence and about Heaven and Grandpa God,' Berenike said.

Dominic's eyes brightened with excitement. 'Grandpa God?' he asked.

'Sure, he's a very big part of the story,' she said.

'Great opener,' Raphael said to Metatron.

The Archangels sat quietly as Berenike began to tell the story of how things came to be. 'It was once written, long, long ago that a group of Archangels, on God's command, protected the Heavens and the Earth and all living creatures within the Universe. The Archangels were created by God and had specific purpose and dominion over different elements of humanity. They all played their parts as teachers and caretakers of humanity and all of God's creations. Jovan, Michael, Gabriel, Metatron, Uriel and Raphael were all under the command of God. Whilst one would become the leader of God's army, another would shine the brightest of them all. He was known as The Morning Star.'

THE END

ABOUT THE AUTHOR

L.A. STAFFORD was born in Sydney, Australia, and grew up in Townsville, North Queensland, just off the coastline near the Great Barrier Reef.

She's a lover of architectural and black and white photography, collector of angel statues, and a lover of the spirit world.

For news and updates and to find out more about L.A. STAFFORD, visit www.lastaffordauthor.com